Dear Friends, P9-EFJ-729

Several years ago I was asked to write a story involving a cat. No problem. As it happened our children have owned several cats through the years. Wayne's and my first pet was a cat named, appropriately enough, Kitty. For the first few years of our marriage it was Cats "R" Us. Then, along with the children, came the hamsters, guinea pigs, several dogs, a snake or two, an injured crow, and even a horse. That was when the household became Animals "R" Us. Four children, born within five years, and an entire menagerie of pets . . . oh, those were the days!

I titled my story *Family Affair* for reasons you will come to understand once you start reading. The book made a small blip in the publishing world and then was laid to rest in the out-of-print section of some computer database until now . . .

Apparently my cat Cleo, the heroine of *Family Affair*, has more than one life. Cleo is back and eager to share her story with you. As you'll soon discover, love in the cat world is almost as complicated as it is with humans.

I hope you enjoy this romantic comedy, raised from the ashes like the phoenix to live and charm again. Pour yourself a cup of tea, cuddle up in a comfortable chair, and if one is at hand, put a cat in your lap to pet while you're reading. I always find it comforting to hold an animal in my lap.

I enjoy hearing from my readers. You can reach me at www.DebbieMacomber.com or by writing me at P.O. Box 1458, Port Orchard, WA 98366.

Warmest regards,
Debbie Macomber

By Debbie Macomber

DEBBIE MACOMBER

Family Affair

AVON

An Imprint of HarperCollinsPublishers

This book was originally published in 1994 as "Family Affair" in *Purrfect Love* by HarperMonogram, an Imprint of HarperCollins Publishers.

"Homemade Treats for Your Cat" appears courtesy of PetPlace.com.

AVON BOOKS
An Imprint of HarperCollins*Publishers*
10 East 53rd Street
New York, New York 10022-5299

Copyright © 1994, 2011 by Debbie Macomber
"The Bet" copyright © 2012 by Darlene Panzera
Excerpts from *A Season of Angels; The Trouble with Angels; Touched by Angels; Mrs. Miracle; Morning Comes Softly; One Night; Someday Soon; Sooner or Later* copyright © 1993, 1994, 1995, 1996 by Debbie Macomber
ISBN 978-0-06-199713-6
www.avonromance.com

First Avon Books mass market printing: July 2012
First William Morrow hardcover printing: January 2011

Avon Trademark Reg. U.S. Pat. Off. and in Other Countries, Marca Registrada, Hecho en U.S.A.
HarperCollins® is a registered trademark of HarperCollins Publishers.

Printed in the U.S.A.

10 9 8 7 6 5 4 3 2 1

To Denise Weyrick
for her love, kindness,
dedication to family and friends,
and courage

Family Affair

One

"I'VE GOT THE BACKBONE OF A WORM," LACEY Lancaster muttered as she let herself into her apartment. She tossed her mail onto an end table and glared at Cleo. "I didn't say a word to Mr. Sullivan, not a single word."

Cleo, her Abyssinian cat, affectionately wove her golden-brown body between Lacey's ankles. Her long tail coiled around Lacey's calf like a feather boa; soft, sleek, and soothing.

"I had the perfect opportunity to ask for a raise and did I do it?" Lacey demanded, kicking her feet so that her shoes sailed in opposite directions. "Oh, no, I let it pass by. And do you know why?"

Cleo apparently didn't. Lacey took off her bright green vinyl raincoat, opened the closet door, and shoved it inside. "Because I'm a coward, that's why."

1

Walking into the kitchen, she opened the refrigerator and stuck her head inside, rooting out some sorry-looking leftovers, two boxes of take-out Chinese, and the tulip bulbs she'd meant to plant in her balcony flower box last October.

"I'm starved." She opened the vegetable bin and took out a limp stalk of celery. "You know my problem, don't you?"

Cleo meowed and wove her way between Lacey's ankles once more.

"Oh, sorry. You're probably hungry too." Lacey reached inside the cupboard and pulled out a can of gourmet cat food. To her surprise, Cleo didn't show the least bit of interest. Instead, she raised her tail and stuck her rear end in the air.

"What's going on with you? Trust me, Cleo, this isn't the time to go all weird on me. I need to talk." Taking her celery stick with her, she moved into the living room and fell onto the love seat.

"I work and slave and put in all kinds of overtime—without pay, I might add—and for what? Mr. Sullivan doesn't appreciate me. Yet it's *my* decorating ideas he uses. The worst part is, he doesn't even bother to give me the credit." She chomped off the end of the celery and chewed with a vengeance. The stalk teetered from the attack and then slowly curved downward.

Lacey studied the celery. "This might as well be my backbone," she muttered. Unable to sit still any longer, she paced her compact living room. "I haven't had a raise in the whole year I've worked for him, and in that time I've taken on much more responsibility and completed projects Mr. Sullivan couldn't or wouldn't do. Good grief, if it weren't for me, Mr. Sullivan wouldn't know what was going on in his own business." By this time she was breathless and irate. "I do more work than he does, and he's the owner, for heaven's sake!"

Clearly Cleo agreed, because she let out a low, wailing moan. Lacey had never owned a cat before, but after a devastating divorce she'd needed someone. Or some thing. The thing had turned out to be Cleo.

She'd first spotted Cleo in a pet-shop window, looking forlorn. Cleo's brother and sister had been sold two weeks earlier, and Cleo was all alone. Abandoned, the half-grown kitten gazed, dejected and miserable, onto the world that passed her by.

Lacey had been suffering from the same emotions herself, and once they met the two had become fast friends. No fool, the pet-store owner knew a sale when he saw one. He'd made some fast soft-shoe moves to convince Lacey what a good investment Cleo would be. If she bred her and sold off the litter, within a year or so, he claimed, her original investment would be returned to her.

Lacey hadn't been so keen on the breeding aspect of the deal, but it had sounded like something she should try. She wanted companionship, and after her disastrous marriage she was through with men. A cat wouldn't lie or cheat or cause hurt. Peter had done all three with bone-cutting accuracy.

Good ol' Peter, Lacey mused. She should be grateful for all the lessons he'd taught her. Perhaps someday she would be able to look back on her marriage without the crushing pain she felt now. He'd vowed to love and cherish her but then calmly announced one Sunday afternoon, without warning, that he was leaving her for someone else.

Someone else was a tall blonde with baby blue eyes and a voluptuous figure. Lacey had sized up the competition, decided she didn't stand a chance, and signed the divorce papers. Oh, there'd been some haggling, but she'd left that to her attorney and stayed out of it as much as possible. As soon as her divorce was final, she'd uprooted herself, moved to San Francisco, located a job she loved, and started life all over again.

Sort of.

This time, she was playing it smart. Men were completely out of the picture. For the first time, she was supporting herself. For the first time, she didn't need anyone else. Because it could happen all over again. Another blonde with a *Playboy* figure could disrupt her life a second time. It was best to play it safe. Who needed that kind of grief? Not her!

Lacey wasn't discounting her assets. With her straight brown hair sculpted around her ears, and equally dark eyes, she resembled a lovable pixie. She was barely five feet tall, while her brother, who was five years older, was nearly six feet. Why nature had short-changed her in the height department, she would never understand.

After the divorce, Lacey had felt emotionally battered and lost. Bringing Cleo into her life had helped tremendously, so much that Lacey figured she could do without a man. Her cat provided all the companionship she needed.

"Okay, okay, you're right," Lacey said, glancing down at her fidgeting feline friend. "I couldn't agree with you more. I'm a gutless wonder. The real problem is I don't want to quit my job. All I'm looking for is to be paid what I'm worth, which is a whole lot more than I'm making now." She'd come out of the divorce with a hefty settlement; otherwise she'd be in dire financial straits.

Cleo concurred with a low wail, unlike any sound Lacey could ever remember her making.

Lacey studied her cat. "You all right, girl? You don't sound right."

Cleo thrust her hind end into the air again and shot across the room to attack her catnip mouse. Whatever was troubling her had passed. At least Lacey hoped it had.

Muttering to herself, Lacey returned to the kitchen and reexamined the contents of her refrigerator. There wasn't anything there she'd seriously consider eating. The leftover Chinese containers were filled with hard, dried-out rice and a thick red sauce with what had once been sweet-and-sour pork. The meat had long since disappeared, and the sauce resembled cherry gelatin. The only edible items were the tulip bulbs, not that she'd seriously consider dining on them.

She'd hoped to treat herself to something extravagant to celebrate her raise. Domino's Pizza was about as extravagant as she got. But she wasn't doing any celebrating this night. If she wanted dinner, she'd need to fix it herself.

Her cupboards weren't promising: a couple of cans of soup mingled with fifteen of gourmet cat food.

Soup.

Her life had deteriorated to a choice between cream of mushroom and vegetarian vegetable. Blindly she reached for a can and brought out the vegetable. The freezer held a loaf of bread. Her choice of sandwiches was limited to either peanut butter and jelly or grilled cheese.

"Sometimes I think I hate you!" The words came through the kitchen wall as clearly as if the person saying them were standing in the same room.

Lacey sighed. Her neighbor, Jack Walker, and his girlfriend were at it again. She hadn't formally met the man who lived next door, which was fine with her. The guy suffered from severe woman problems; from what she'd heard through the wall, it sounded as if the pair was badly in need of therapy. Lacey avoided Jack like the plague, despite his numerous attempts at striking up an acquaintance. She was polite but firm, even discouraging. She had to give him credit. He didn't accept *no* easily. Over the months, his methods had become increasingly imaginative. He'd tried flowers, tacked notes to her door, and had once attempted to lure her into his apartment with the offer of dinner. Of all his tactics, the promise of a meal had been the most tempting, but Lacey knew trouble when she saw it and resisted.

As far as she was concerned, dating Jack was out of the question, especially since he was already involved with someone else. Lacey had lost count of the times she'd heard him arguing with his girlfriend. Some nights she was forced to turn on her stereo to block out the noise.

But being the polite, don't-cause-problems

sort of person she was, Lacey had never complained. She might as well throw herself down on the carpet and instruct people to walk all over her.

"I wasn't always a worm," she complained to Cleo. "It's only in the last year or so that I've lost my self-confidence. I'd like to blame Mr. Sullivan, but I can't. Not when I'm the one who's at fault. You'd think it'd be easy to ask for a little thing like a raise, wouldn't you? It isn't, yet I'm left feeling like Oliver Twist. At least he had the courage to ask for more.

"Mr. Sullivan should thank his lucky stars. I'm good at what I do, but does he notice? Oh, no. He just takes me for granted."

Having finished this tirade, she noticed that Cleo had disappeared. Even her cat had deserted her. She found Cleo on the windowsill, meowing pathetically.

Lacey lifted the cat in her arms and petted her. "Have I been so wrapped up in my own problems that I've ignored you?"

Cleo leaped out of the embrace and raced into the bedroom.

The arguing continued in the other apartment.

"Sarah, for the love of heaven, be reasonable!" Jack shouted.

"Give it to him with both barrels," Lacey said under her breath. "I bet you didn't know Jack was dating on the side, did you? Well, don't get down on yourself. I didn't know what a womanizer Peter was either."

Sarah apparently heeded her advice, because the shouting intensified. Jack, who generally remained the calmer of the two, was also losing it.

If she listened real hard, she might be able to figure out the cause of their dispute, but frankly Lacey wasn't that interested.

"I saw him with someone new just last week," she added, just for fun. Lacey had bumped into Jack at the mailbox. There'd been a woman with him and it wasn't Sarah. But it was always Sarah who came back. Always Sarah he quarreled with. The poor girl apparently cared deeply for him. More fool she.

"I'm having vegetarian vegetable soup," Lacey informed Cleo as she strolled into the room, thinking her pet would want to know. "It isn't anything that would interest you, unfortunately." Whatever had been troubling her cat earlier was under control for the moment.

Dinner complete, Lacey set her steaming bowl of soup and her grilled cheese sandwich on the table. She'd just sat down when something hit the wall in the apartment next door. Instinctively, she jumped.

Angry voices escalated. Jack was no longer calm and in control. In fact, it sounded as if he'd lost his cool completely. The two were shouting at each other, each trying to drown the other out.

Lacey sighed. Enough was enough. Setting her napkin aside, she went over to the kitchen wall and knocked politely. Either they didn't hear her or they chose to ignore her, something they did with increasing frequency.

She'd just sat down again when an explosion of noise nearly jerked her off the chair. One or the other of the disgruntled lovers had decided to turn on the radio. Full blast.

The radio was turned off as abruptly as it had been turned on, followed by a tirade from Jack.

The radio was switched back on.

Off.

Once again, ever so politely, Lacey tapped the wall.

They ignored her.

Then, for whatever reason, there was silence. Blissful silence. Whatever had plagued the two was settled. Either that or they'd murdered one another. Whichever it was, the silence was bliss.

When Lacey had finished her dinner, she washed the few dishes she'd used. Cleo continued to weave her sleek body between Lacey's ankles, meowing and wailing all the while. "What's wrong with you, girl?" Lacey asked again.

Squatting down, she ran her hand over the cat's spine. Cleo arched her back and cried once more.

"You don't seem to be yourself," Lacey commented, concerned.

It hit her then, right between the eyes. "You're in heat! Oh, my goodness, you're in heat." How could she have been so obtuse?

Leaving the kitchen, she rooted through her personal telephone directory, searching for the name the pet-shop owner had given her. If she was going to breed Cleo, she needed to talk to this woman first.

"Poor, poor Cleo," Lacey said sympathetically. "Trust me, sweetie, men aren't worth all this trouble." She quickly located the phone number and punched it out.

"I'm Lacey Lancaster," she said hurriedly into the receiver. "The owner of Pet's World gave me your number. I bought an Abyssinian several months ago."

No sooner had she introduced herself when the arguing in the next-door apartment resumed.

"I'm sorry, dearie, but I can't understand you." The woman on the other end of the line spoke with a soft Irish accent.

"I said I purchased an Abyssinian cat—"

"It sounds like you've a party going on."

"There's no party." Lacey spoke louder, close to shouting herself.

"Perhaps you should call me back when your guests have left," came the soft Irish brogue. With that the line was disconnected.

Something snapped in Lacey. Her never-cause-a-scene upbringing went down the drain faster than tap water. She slammed the phone down and clenched her fists.

"I've had it!" she shouted. And she had. With men who didn't know the meaning of the words "faithful" and "commitment." With employers who took advantage of their employees. With Neanderthal neighbors, who shuffled one woman after another through their apartments without a second thought.

Lacey walked out her door and down the hall, her strides eating up the distance in seconds. However, by the time she reached Jack's apartment the fire had died down. Her anger would solve nothing. She tapped politely and waited.

The arguing stopped abruptly and the door flew open. Lacey was so astonished that she leaped back. Sarah leaped back, too, and glared at her. It was apparent the other woman hadn't heard Lacey knock.

"Hello," Lacey said, her heartbeat roaring in her ears. "I was wondering if you two would mind holding it down just a little bit."

The woman, young and pretty, blinked back tears. "You don't need to worry. I was just leaving!"

Jack appeared then, looking suave and composed. He brightened when he saw it was her. "Lacey," he said, flashing her an easy grin. "This is a pleasant surprise."

"With all your fighting, I couldn't even make a phone call," she explained, not wanting to give him the wrong impression. This wasn't a social visit.

"I apologize." Jack glared at Sarah. "It won't happen again."

Sarah's chin shot into the air as she jerked her purse strap over her shoulder. "I . . . I don't believe we have anything more to say to each other." She hurried past Lacey toward the elevator.

"Sarah." Jack placed both his hands on Lacey's shoulders and edged his way past her. "I'm warning you . . . just don't do anything stupid."

"You mean, like listen to you?"

Jack groaned and stared at Lacey as if this were all her fault.

Lacey opened her mouth to tell him exactly what she thought of him and then abruptly changed her mind. Jack wouldn't listen. Men never did. Why waste her breath?

With nothing more to say, she returned to her apartment. To her surprise she realized she'd left the door open. Her immediate concern was for Cleo, and she rushed inside in a panic.

She stopped cold in her tracks at the sight that greeted her.

"Cleo!" Her cat was in the throes of passion with a long-haired feline she didn't recognize.

Placing her hands over her mouth, Lacey sagged against the wall. She wasn't going to need the Irish woman after all. Cleo had already found her mate.

Two

"S TOP!" LACEY DEMANDED, ALREADY KNOWING it was too late. The two cats ignored her. So much for the thrill of being a cat owner.

Knowing only one thing to do, Lacey raced into the kitchen and filled a tall glass with water. She'd get the lovers' attention soon enough. Rushing back into the living room, she tripped on a throw rug and staggered a few steps in a desperate effort to maintain her balance. By the time she reached the cats, most of the liquid was down the front of her blouse and only a few drops landed on the passionate couple.

By then they were finished and the strange cat was looking for a way out of her apartment. Typical male! He'd gotten what he wanted and was ready to be on his merry way.

Lacey was about to open the sliding glass

door that led out to her balcony when someone rang her doorbell. Frowning fiercely at the alley cat, Lacey traipsed across her living room and checked the peephole.

It was her Don Juan neighbor, fresh from his argument with Sarah. "Hello again." He flashed her an easy smile which, Lacey hated to admit, hit its mark. She didn't know what was in her personality profile that made her vulnerable to this type of man, but whatever it was, she sincerely wished it would go away.

"I don't suppose you've seen my cat?" he asked.

"You own a cat?"

"Actually, he allows me to live with him."

As if she'd planned it this way, Cleo strolled past, her tail in the air, giving the impression of royalty. The long-haired mixed breed followed closely behind, looking as if he'd rested enough for a second go-round.

"There's Dog," Jack said.

"Dog? You named your cat Dog?"

"Yeah," he said, walking past her. He reached for his cat affectionately and cradled him in his arms. "I wanted a dog, but I had to compromise."

"So you got yourself a cat named Dog." In light of how she'd met his faithful companion, Lacey wasn't amused.

"Exactly."

"Well, listen here, your Dog has stolen Cleo's virginity. What do you plan to do about it?"

Jack's eyes widened. Lacey swore the man looked downright pleased. "Dog? What do you have to say for yourself?"

"It's you I'm asking," Lacey said, squaring her shoulders. "As a responsible pet owner, you have an answer, I hope."

His dark eyes narrowed. "I can only apologize."

"Then I accept your apology," Lacey murmured. It seemed darn little in light of the possible consequences, but the less they had to say to each other the better. Lacey wanted as little to do with Jack as possible. The more she saw of him the more attracted she was, which made absolutely no sense. She was like someone on a strict diet, irresistibly drawn to a dessert tray.

"Listen, I was hoping for an opportunity to get to know you a little better," Jack said, as if he planned to stay awhile.

Lacey couldn't allow that to happen. She all but opened the door for him.

"We've been neighbors for the past several months. I think we must have gotten started on the wrong foot," he said, showing no signs of leaving. "I understand you aren't interested in dating, but we could be a bit more neighborly, don't you think?"

Lacey nodded politely, if reluctantly. It would help to have someone to feed her cat and collect her mail on occasion. She would be willing to do the same for him, but she wanted it firmly understood that this was the extent of what she was offering.

She told him so.

"Friends?" he asked, holding out his hand.

"Friends," she agreed. They exchanged handshakes. She found his grasp secure, but his fingers held hers far longer than necessary. She disliked the way her heart reacted. This man was dangerous in more ways than one. The less she had to do with him, the better.

He seemed to be waiting for her to invite him to stay for coffee and chitchat. The thought was tempting. It would be nice to have someone to be neighborly with, but the lesson she'd learned from Peter had sunk in.

"We do seem to share a love of cats," Jack added, as if this were grounds for a long-standing friendship.

"I like Cleo," she said pointedly. "Now if you'll excuse me." This time she held the door open for him.

"It was nice talking to you, Lacey," Jack said with a boyish grin that was potent enough to topple her resolve to limit their relationship. "I'm hoping we can become *good* friends."

Lacey didn't miss the emphasis on *good*. The last thing she needed or wanted was friendship with a known Casanova. Not when she'd been fool enough to marry one who'd ruthlessly left her for another.

Since she hadn't summoned the gumption to ask for a raise, she found it even more difficult to explain to her neighbor that she wasn't interested in a man who kept women on the side.

Jack left then, to Lacey's intense relief. She scooped Cleo up in her arms and held her tight, as if her beloved cat had had a narrow escape.

Cleo, however, didn't take kindly to being pressed against a wet blouse and squirmed free, leaping onto the carpet. She made her way to the seat of the overstuffed chair, her favorite spot for a catnap, and curled up contentedly. It might have been Lacey's imagination, but Cleo seemed completely at ease and thoroughly satisfied.

Just as Lacey was about to turn on the television, the phone rang. It was probably her best friend, Jeanne Becker. Jeanne had been one of the first people to befriend Lacey after her move to San Francisco. She worked as a dental assistant and was single, like Lacey, but had been dating Dave steadily for nearly a year. However, neither seemed to be in any hurry to get engaged. With so many friends divorcing, they both wanted to be very sure they were taking the right step.

"Well?" Jeanne asked. "Did you ask for your raise?"

"No," Lacey confessed.

"Why not?" Jeanne demanded. "You promised you would. What's so difficult about talking to Mr. Sullivan?"

"I have no defense. I'm a worm."

"What are you so frightened of?" Jeanne

asked after a thoughtful moment, as if there were something deep and dark hidden in Lacey's childhood that kept her from confronting her employer.

"I don't know," Lacey admitted. "It's just that Mr. Sullivan is so . . . so intimidating. He's got these beady eyes, and when I ask to talk to him, he looks at his watch as if he doesn't have any time for me and asks how long it will take. And by the time he goes through this little routine, I've lost my nerve."

"Don't you know the man's psyching you out?"

"Yeah, I suppose," Lacey murmured, disheartened. "But knowing that doesn't do any good. My talk with Mr. Sullivan isn't the only thing that went wrong," she added. "Cleo's in heat, and the neighbor's cat stole into my apartment, and I found them . . . together."

"Oh, dear, it sounds like you've had a full day."

"It gets better," Lacey said. "The guy who lives next to me suggested we be neighborly."

"You mean the hunk who's been asking you out for the last six months? I met him, remember?"

Lacey wasn't comfortable thinking of Jack in those terms, but she let her friend's comment pass. "Yeah. He owns Dog, the cat who had his way with Cleo. And before you ask, I did get the name of his cat right."

"I could like this guy," Jeanne said, laughing softly.

"You're welcome to him."

"Lacey! Honestly, when are you going to let bygones be bygones? Peter was a rat, but he's out of your life. The worst thing you can do is blame other men for what happened between you and your ex."

"I'm not blaming other men."

"You've been divorced for over a year now and you never date."

"I don't want another relationship."

"You were wise not to date right away," Jeanne said sympathetically, "but now it's time you got on with your life. If you want my advice, I think you should go out with Jack. He's adorable."

"Are you crazy?" Lacey insisted. "He was fighting with Sarah again. It's all I can do not to tell that sweet young girl what I know. He's playing her for a fool just the way Peter played me."

"You're jumping to conclusions."

"I don't think so," Lacey insisted. "They're constantly fighting. From bits of conversation I've heard, it sounds like Jack wants her to move in with him. Apparently she's on to him because she refuses. I wouldn't trust him either."

"You know what's happened, don't you?" Jeanne asked. "You've gotten to be a cynic. I don't think you realize how much Peter hurt you."

"Nonsense," was Lacey's immediate reply. "He didn't do anything more than teach me a valuable lesson."

❖   ❖   ❖

LACEY DIDN'T SLEEP WELL THAT NIGHT. IT WAS LITTLE wonder, in light of how her day had gone. The unpleasant run-in with her neighbor continued to plague her. Jack was easygoing and friendly, the kind of man who put people at ease. Not her, though. Lacey's defenses went up whenever he was around her.

As luck would have it, they met in the hallway on their way to work the following morning.

"Off to the coal mines, I see," he said amicably as they made their way to the elevator. He was dressed in a dark three-piece suit, and the only word she could think to describe him was debonair. His smile was wide and charming. Too charming, Lacey decided. His eyes were friendly and warm, the type of eyes a woman remembers for a long time.

"Where do you work?" he asked conversationally as he summoned the elevator.

"Sullivan's Decorating," she answered, without elaborating. Encouraging conversation between them wouldn't be smart. It would be far too easy to be seduced by his magnetism.

"Really? I think that was the firm the bank hired last year when we redecorated."

"We've been involved in several bank renovations," she agreed evenly. So Jack was a bank executive? Lacey didn't press for information, although she couldn't help being curious.

As if reading her thoughts, he reached inside his suit pocket and handed her a business card. "Come see me if you ever need a loan."

"I will, thank you."

"I'll look forward to having you apply." He smiled down on her and, even knowing what she did about him, her heart fluttered. She was cursed, Lacey mused, destined to be attracted to the wrong kind of men. There was probably some technical name for it, some term psychologists used for women like her. *Nutty* would do, she decided. Tangling her life with his would be downright disastrous.

"Have a good day," Jack said when the elevator opened.

"You too." Her voice was little more than a whisper.

"Say," Jack said, turning back abruptly, as if struck by inspiration. "I don't suppose you'd be free for dinner tomorrow night?"

Instinctively, Lacey stiffened. So he hadn't given up trying. "No . . . I'm sorry, I'm not free," she said. Apparently she conveyed her message because he didn't press her.

He glanced at his watch and frowned. "Perhaps another time."

"Perhaps."

Lacey wasn't making Jack Walker any promises. But she couldn't get the thought of Jack out of her mind all day.

❁   ❁   ❁

THE FOLLOWING EVENING, WHEN LACEY WAS TAKING her trash to the chute at the end of the hallway, she ran into Jack a second time, just as he was going out his door.

Taken by surprise, they stopped and stared at each other. He was dressed formally as if for a fancy dinner date. Lacey didn't need to be reminded that he could have been wining and dining her. She'd declined his offhand invitation, but she wished briefly that she'd accepted. Then she decided she was right to refuse. There were probably any number of other women who struck his fancy. Then, too, there was always Sarah. Ever loyal, ever faithful.

"Hello again," Jack said, with his electric smile.

"Hello." Her voice sounded awkward. Stilted.

"How's it going?"

"Fine." She didn't ask about him. The answer was obvious. He looked wonderful. Bank executives shouldn't be this good-looking or this friendly.

"Here, let me help." He took the plastic garbage can out of her hand.

"I can do that." Nevertheless, she was pleased he offered.

"I'm sure you can, but let me play the role of gentleman. It'd make my mama proud." The smile was back in place, potent enough to melt away the strongest of resolves. Hers, unfortunately, dissolved faster than most.

They went down the hallway together. Lacey took pains to avoid brushing shoulders with him. "Thanks for the help," she said, when they neared her apartment door.

"No problem. I was happy to do it."

She reached for the doorknob, intent on escaping. "Have a good time," she said, turning her back to him.

"I probably won't," he said softly, "especially since I won't be spending the evening with you. I'm destined to sit through a boring dinner meeting. I wish you could have seen your way clear to go with me."

"I—" She was so flustered by his sweet talk she could barely speak. "I'm sure you'll have an enjoyable evening. Will you be seeing Sarah?" she added, not knowing where the courage came to ask the question. Sarah was the one he should have invited, not her.

"Not tonight," he said. "I'm afraid I'm stuck with my assistant."

First he'd invited her, and when she refused he'd asked his assistant. Suddenly Lacey was furious. That was exactly what she expected of someone like Jack. Someone like Peter.

Poor Sarah was destined for a broken heart.

Three

CLEO'S PREGNANT," LACEY MOANED AS SHE slumped into the BART seat next to Jeanne two weeks later. "I took her to the vet yesterday afternoon and he confirmed her condition." Lacey was deeply dismayed that her purebred Abyssinian had mated with Jack's tomcat. And her dissatisfaction with her neighbor didn't stop there.

Sarah had stopped by over the past weekend, and the sounds of their argument had come through the walls again. Both had been furious. This time, however, they kept the intensity of their disagreement to a lower pitch, and their fight didn't last long. No more than ten minutes had elapsed before Lacey heard Jack's apartment door slam and Sarah's footsteps hurrying down the hall. Jack had stuck his head out and called after her, but to no avail.

"What are you going to do about Cleo?" Jeanne wanted to know.

"I . . . I haven't decided yet." Several options were open to her, but one thing was certain: she was determined that Jack accept some responsibility.

❀   ❀   ❀

THAT EVENING, AFTER WORK, WITH HER HEART IN her throat, Lacey approached Jack's door and knocked three times in hard, timed beats.

"Lacey, hello! This is a pleasant surprise."

"Hello," she said stiffly. "Would you mind if I came in for a moment?"

"Not at all. I'd be honored." He stepped aside and let her into the living room, which was more than double the size of her own. "Can I get you something to drink?" he asked.

"Nothing, thanks." She sat down on a white leather sofa and took a small notebook from her purse. "I'm afraid this isn't a social call."

Jack sank into a recliner opposite her. He perched close to the edge of the seat cushion and braced his elbows against his knees. "Is there a problem?"

"As a matter of fact, there is," Lacey answered. "Dog got Cleo pregnant."

"I see."

"I thought you should know."

"Yes, of course." He looked as if he were entirely in the dark as to what she wanted from him. "Is there something you needed?" he asked after an awkward moment.

How like a man! "Yes," she said, having trouble restraining her irritation. "I want you to do right by my cat."

"Do right? Are you suggesting they marry?"

"Don't be ridiculous!"

"Then what do you mean?"

"It's only fair that you share the expenses with me." She hated the way her voice trembled. "Dr. Christman, Cleo's vet, prescribed expensive vitamins and another checkup. In addition, I'll expect you to find homes for your half of the litter."

"My half."

"Yes. Please submit the names to me for approval."

Jack scratched the side of his head. "You're serious about this, aren't you?"

That he should question her motives told her everything she needed to know about him. "Yes, I'm serious. Dead serious." She stood and handed him a list of her expenses so far. "You can pay me whenever it's convenient." Holding her purse against her chest as though it offered her protection, she kept her back ramrod straight. "There are consequences in owning an alley cat, Mr. Walker. Even one named Dog." Lacey knew how pious she sounded. Lines of righteousness creased her face as she let herself out.

She didn't realize how badly she was shaking until she was inside her own apartment. Her knees felt as if they were about to buckle. She sat on the love seat and Cleo leaped into her lap, eager for attention.

Lacey ran her hand down the length of Cleo's back. "Well, girl, you're going to be a mother. What do you think about that?"

Cleo meowed.

"This is destined to be an interesting couple of months," she said. Dr. Christman had given Lacey several pamphlets about the reproduction of cats. Lacey had read them a number of times. She'd grown up with a gentle cocker spaniel named Sherlock, but he'd been a male so she'd never been through this sort of thing.

❈   ❈   ❈

THE FOLLOWING AFTERNOON, LACEY'S DOORBELL rang. Jack was on the other side, leaning against the doorjamb. He gave her a slow, easy, heart-stopping grin.

"How's Cleo doing?"

"Fine. She seems to need a bit more attention these days, but other than that she's behaving normally."

"I had Dog neutered. He's keeping a low profile these days."

Lacey was forced to pinch her lips together to keep from smiling. As far as she was concerned, it would do Dog good to have his carousing ways curtailed.

"May I come in?"

Lacey wasn't sure letting Jack into her apartment was such a good idea. "All right," she said reluctantly, stepping aside.

Then Lacey made the mistake of politely asking if he'd like something to drink, and Jack asked for coffee. Since she didn't have any ready, she was required to assemble a pot.

To her dismay, Jack was intent on helping her. She turned on the water and measured out the coffee grounds, all the while complaining inwardly about her compact kitchen. She couldn't move without touching Jack in some way. When she stood on tiptoe to lift down the mugs, he stepped behind her, the full length of his body pressing against hers.

She felt trapped and silly and unbearably uncomfortable. Worse, she was blushing, although she did everything she could to disguise the effect he had on her.

"It seems only fair if I'm going to share the expenses of Cleo's pregnancy that I have visitation rights," he said casually.

A chill washed over her. "Visitation rights?"

"Yes. I'd like to check on her every now and again to be sure she's doing well."

Lacey wasn't sure this was such a good idea, either, but she couldn't think of any good reason to protest.

"I can assure you Cleo will be well cared for."

"I'm confident she will be, but I'd like to check on her myself."

"All right," she agreed with ill grace.

The coffee finished brewing and she poured

them each a cup. Jack took his black and strong, but he waited while Lacey diluted hers with milk before returning to the living room.

Cleo walked regally into the room and without a pause jumped into Jack's lap. Lacey was amazed. Her cat had never been fond of strangers.

"Cleo," Lacey chastised. "Get down."

The cat would have been a fool to do so. Jack was petting her back in long, smooth strokes that left Cleo purring with delight. It was probably like this with every woman he touched. Lacey attempted to scrounge up resentment toward him, and to her amazement found she couldn't.

Instead, the very opposite was happening. It was as if Jack's hands were on Lacey. A series of warm, dizzy sensations began to grow in her. Sexual feelings. Her breath came in little short puffs. She sipped at her coffee and forced herself to look away, anything that would make this feeling disappear. It was much too uncomfortable to remember that part of her nature, the one she'd buried after her divorce and conveniently ignored until Jack walked into her life.

Looking away didn't help. Nothing did.

"Cleo's a beautiful cat," he said in a low, sexy drawl that had Cleo purring and Lacey's heart racing.

"Thank you," she managed.

The tingling feeling spread slowly, inexorably, through her body, leaving her with a need she wouldn't have dared express to another human being. It had been well over a year since a man had held her. Not once in all those months had she missed a man's touch. Until now.

Now it was torture to sit and do nothing. To her dismay, Jack seemed relaxed and in no hurry to leave.

"Have you thought about homes for your half of the litter?" she asked, to make conversation.

"No."

"I . . . I think my friend Jeanne will take one." Her gaze followed the movement of his hand against Cleo's soft fur. The brush of his fingers was light, gentle. A lover's touch. He would be a tender lover, Lacey mused.

She shook her head, needing to clear her

mind before it completed the picture of making love with him. Oh, dear heaven, this was more than she could bear.

"Lacey." The sexy drawl was back. "Come here."

"W-why?"

"I want you to feel Cleo's tummy."

"It's much too soon for the kittens," she protested and all but vaulted out of her chair. He knew exactly what he was doing to her and he enjoyed it. Lacey's cheeks flamed.

She hurried into the kitchen. Running the faucet, she filled a sponge and wiped down her spotless counter. If only Jack would leave! But that would be asking for a miracle. He had her on the run and wasn't about to give up.

He moved into the compact kitchen, and she closed her eyes, praying for strength.

"It was nice of you to stop by." She hoped he'd leave before she made a fool of herself.

"Why did you turn down my invitation to dinner?" he asked.

She swore he was only inches behind her, but she didn't dare turn around.

"Lacey?"

She opened the cupboard and brought down a can of cat food. "I don't think it's a good idea for us to become involved."

"Why not?"

"It's fine to be neighborly, but . . ."

"Not too friendly."

"Exactly." Her heart continued to beat at maximum speed, clamoring loudly in her ear. She didn't dare look at him. She couldn't, without his knowing that she wasn't any better off than Cleo was with Dog.

"Turn around and look at me," he instructed her gently, and when she didn't comply he placed his hands on her shoulders and slowly moved her to face him. Then he ran his thumb along the edge of her jaw. "Look at me," he repeated.

Lacey closed her eyes and lowered her head. "I think you should leave."

Using his thumb, he lifted her chin. "Open your eyes."

She had no choice but to do as he asked. Reluctantly her eyes opened and slid effortlessly to his.

"I remember the day you moved in." He spoke softly, clearly. His gaze was as dark and intense as she'd ever seen. "I realized then how badly I wanted to get to know you. There was something vulnerable about you. Something that told me I would need to be patient; and so I've bided my time. It's been a year now and I'm still waiting, but I'm growing restless."

Lacey's throat felt dry, and she doubted she could have spoken even if she'd wanted to. Which she didn't. What could she say? That she'd once trusted someone who'd destroyed her faith in all men?

"Who hurt you?" he asked.

She shook her head, unwilling to answer him.

He took her in his arms then, drawing her into a protective circle, easing her into his embrace. His hold was loose, comforting, seductive.

Lacey wanted to resist, tried to make herself pull away, and found she couldn't.

"I want to kiss you," he whispered, as if he felt he needed to warn her of every move he made for fear she'd bolt and run like a frightened rabbit.

"No." She shook her head wildly from side to side. Somehow she found the resistance to brace her hands against his forearms and push herself away.

He let go of her instantly, but hesistantly. "Why not?" he asked. "I would never hurt you, Lacey. I'd never do anything you didn't want, weren't ready for."

"You must think me a fool," she said, her breasts heaving with the effort it had cost her to walk away from him.

"A fool?"

"You love Sarah."

"Of course I love Sarah."

At least he didn't deny it. "How many other women do you have on a string? Don't answer that; I don't want to know. Just understand one thing. I refuse to be one of them."

"Lacey."

"Please leave." She folded her arms and thrust out her chin defiantly.

"Not until you listen to me."

"You can't say anything that will change my mind."

His laugh mocked her. "Not even when I tell you Sarah's my sister?"

Four

YOUR SISTER!" LACEY REPEATED, STUNNED. For a moment she wondered if she could trust Jack to tell her the truth but then decided she could. The intimacy between Jack and Sarah was what had struck her the first time she'd seen them together. It made sense that they were brother and sister.

"Who did you think she was?" Jack demanded. "You assumed Sarah and I were lovers? How could you possibly think something like that?"

"You're constantly fighting, and—"

"Of course we fight, we're siblings. Sarah's living with a man and I don't approve. I wish she'd use the brains God gave her and get out."

"Do you disapprove of their living arrangement or of the young man?" Lacey wanted to know.

"Both. As far as I'm concerned, she's making the biggest mistake of her life. Mom and Dad don't know, and I refuse to hide it from them much longer."

"*That's* the reason you keep insisting she move in with you!" Lacey had caught the gist of their disagreement several times and cheered when Sarah flatly refused him. This new information put a different slant on Sarah's refusal.

"How do you know what we argue about?" he asked, regarding her quizzically.

"You honestly think I can't hear you two? Those walls are made of papier-mâché." Her head was reeling. If Sarah was Jack's sister, that answered a multitude of awkward questions.

Jack stuffed his hands in his pockets and strolled to the far side of the kitchen. His brow creased as if he were deep in thought. "I didn't realize we'd been quite so loud."

"You both certainly seem to have strong feelings on the subject."

"All this time you believed I was two-timing Sarah?"

"What else was I to think?" she asked defensively. "Besides, there were all those other women."

"What other women?"

"The one I saw you with the other day at the mailbox, for example."

"You mean Gloria?"

"I didn't hear her name. . . . Listen, none of this matters. You're free to date whomever you want. You don't owe me any explanations."

He didn't seem to hear her. "Gloria's a friend, nothing more. We did date a few years back, but it didn't develop into anything. She's seeing someone else now."

"What about your assistant?" Lacey asked, before she could censor the question.

"Mrs. Blake?" He laughed outright. "She's fifty and a grandmother."

Lacey wanted so badly to believe him. "Fifty?"

He nodded. "There's only one woman I've had my eye on for the last several months, and it's you."

"You talk a sweet line, Jack Walker, but I've heard it all before." More times than she cared to count. More times than she wanted to remember.

He raised an eyebrow as he advanced a couple of steps toward her. "If you let me kiss you, who knows? You just might change your mind."

The temptation was strong, stronger than Lacey wanted it to be. "Another time," she said, her heart roaring in her ears as she backed away from him.

Jack looked disappointed. "All right, Lacey, I've been patient this long. I can wait." He checked his watch and sighed. "I'd better get back to my place. I'll stop by later in the week to check on Cleo." He waited as if he half expected her to protest.

She didn't, although she probably should have. Life had taught her that men weren't to be trusted. Everything Jack said was well and good, but she refused to believe he'd been interested in her all these months. No man had that kind of patience. At least none she'd ever met.

Before he left, he took her by the shoulders and gently planted a kiss on her cheek.

❖   ❖   ❖

"Are you going to go out with Jack?" Jeanne asked when they met the next morning. Lacey's arms were loaded down with several large books of carpet samples. She swore they weighed twenty pounds each. Her arms felt like they were about to come out of their sockets.

"I don't know."

Jeanne eyed her speculatively. "Lacey, you can't let an opportunity like this pass you by. As I said before, the guy's a hunk."

"Handsome isn't everything."

"True, but it's a good start. Besides, I *like* Jack."

"You only met him once."

"True, but I liked what I saw."

Lacey didn't have an answer for that. They rode in silence for several moments.

"I see you brought your work home with you again." Jeanne glanced disapprovingly in the direction of the samples.

"We're making a bid for an accountant's office, and I stopped off on my way home last night and let him look over the different carpets and colors."

"More overtime you're not getting paid for," Jeanne murmured. "Did you ever stop to think what Mr. Sullivan would do without you?"

Lacey had given that question ample consideration. Every time she worked up a quote or dealt with a moody customer because Mr.

Sullivan was "out of the office at the moment," she had that very thought. "He'd probably find some other schmuck to take my place."

"Don't be ridiculous," Jeanne said. "The man needs you. He knows it, and so do you. What you should do, my friend, is use this to your advantage. We both know you should be making double what you make now."

"Double?"

"I don't know what Scrooge is paying you, but I do know it isn't enough. If you don't say something to him soon, I will."

"Jeanne!"

"Relax. I won't. But it makes me angry the way you let him take advantage of you. I don't know what it is about you that lets him get away with it. Do you enjoy being a victim?"

"No!"

Jeanne shrugged. "Then do something about it."

Her friend was right. More than right. She was acting like a victim. Lacey left the BART station filled with indignation. It lasted until she reached the office.

Unfortunately, the lone elevator was out of order. Lugging the carpet samples with her,

Lacey huffed and puffed up three flights of stairs and literally staggered into the office.

Mr. Sullivan glanced up and gave her a look of concern. In his late forties, he was fast going bald, and his blue eyes had faded over the years. His suits were meticulously tailored, though, and he insisted they both maintain a crisp professional image.

Lacey pressed her hand over her heart and slumped into the first available chair.

"Lacey, are you all right?"

She shook her head. She hadn't realized how badly out of shape she was until she'd trekked up those stairs hauling two twenty-pound books of samples.

Mr. Sullivan walked over to the water cooler and drew her a cup of clear cold liquid. "Drink this and you'll feel better."

"Mr. Sullivan . . ."—she was so winded her voice could barely be heard—"we need . . . to talk . . . about my . . . position here."

"Of course. You've done a wonderful job. I owe you a debt of thanks. I realize I've left you with some of the more unpleasant tasks lately, and I hope you'll forgive me for that."

He was a kindly man, she realized. Dissatisfied with her wages, she'd built him up in her mind as an ogre with few redeeming qualities. Much as she'd pictured Jack . . . until recently.

"Overtime?" Her lungs hurt, otherwise she would have elaborated.

He frowned as if he didn't understand her. "Are you saying that over time you'd like to become a full-fledged decorator?"

She nodded, but it was more than that.

"You're wonderfully talented, Lacey. In a couple of years I feel strongly that you'll make it." Having said that, he lifted the heavy sample books, replaced them against the wall, and returned to his desk.

Mumbling under her breath, Lacey walked over to her own desk. No sooner had she removed her jacket than Mr. Sullivan announced he was leaving for the rest of the morning. He didn't tell her where he was headed, which was typical.

❧   ❧   ❧

WHEN LACEY RETURNED TO HER APARTMENT THAT evening, the first thing she did was soak in a hot tub. It felt wonderful.

Her day had been hectic. She certainly

wasn't in the mood for company when there was a knock on her door. She jerked on a pair of sweats. "Oh, please, make this fast," she muttered as she went to answer it.

Jack stood with Sarah on the other side. "I thought it was time the two of you met," he said.

"I'm Sarah," the pretty brunette said, holding out her hand. Now that Lacey knew they were brother and sister, it was easy to see the family resemblance. Sarah shared Jack's deep chocolate-brown eyes and thick dark hair.

"Jack said there'd been a misunderstanding." Sarah grinned as if amused.

"Please make yourselves at home," Lacey said, gesturing toward the living room.

Jack needed no further invitation. He helped himself to the love seat, and Cleo immediately snuggled in his lap as if she'd been waiting for his return.

Lacey and Sarah sat down too.

"I'm sorry for all the commotion Jack and I make," Sarah said. "He's pretty stubborn, you know."

"Me?" Jack protested.

"All right, we both are. Since Mom and Dad

51

moved to Flagstaff, he's the only family I have here in San Francisco. We fight a lot, but we're close too."

"We'd argue a lot less if it wasn't for Mark," Jack said with a frown, eyeing his sister.

Sarah's jaw went tight. "Jack, please, you promised not to bring him up. At any rate," she continued, "I wanted to clear up any misconceptions you might have about me. Jack really is my brother."

"I should have realized that. There's a strong family resemblance."

Sarah stood. "I really need to go—Mark's meeting me for dinner—but I wanted to stop by and introduce myself. Jack's mentioned you several times and—well, I hope everything works out—with Cleo." She squeezed the last two words together in her rush to clarify her meaning.

Sarah left, but Jack stayed exactly where he was—on her love seat with Cleo snoozing contentedly in his lap. "All right," he said, after Lacey had seen Sarah to the door. "What's wrong?"

"What do you mean?"

"Something's troubling you," he said evenly, studying her.

Uncomfortable under his scrutiny, she debated whether or not to tell him the truth. The hot bath hadn't helped to soothe her mind the way she had hoped, and she couldn't stop thinking about what Jeanne had said about her choosing to be a victim.

"I'm a worm," she confessed, slumping in her chair.

"A worm," Jack repeated slowly, as if he wasn't sure of the word's meaning. "In what way?"

She tossed her hands in the air, not wanting to discuss it. The more she complained, the worse she felt. If she was going to whine about her job, she should be doing it to Mr. Sullivan. So far he was the last person to know how she felt, and she had no one to blame but herself.

"All right, you're a worm," Jack said, "but even a worm needs to eat. How about dinner?"

"Out?"

"We can order in if you want, but I bet a night in Chinatown would do us both a world of good."

Lacey blinked back her surprise. Jack was asking her to dinner and she found that she longed to accept more than she had wanted

anything for a long time. Before she could res-
urrect a long list of objections, she nodded.

His smile rivaled the northern lights.
"Great." Gently he set Cleo aside. "You like Chinese food?"

"I love it. Hot and spicy and lots of it."

"Me too. The spicier the better."

"They can't make it too hot for me," she
told him.

He cocked an eyebrow. "Wanna bet?"

Lacey didn't. Jack insisted on a taxi to save
hunting for a parking space in crowded Chinatown. Lacey would have been comfortable
riding BART. She didn't own a car and her only
means of getting around was public transpor-
tation. Luckily the City by the Bay had an excellent metro system.

The taxi let them off on Grant Avenue. Lacey
loved walking along the busy streets of Chinatown. Goods from the small shops spilled onto
the sidewalk, displayed on long narrow tables.
The smells tantalized her. Incense blended
with simmering duck and mingled with the
keen scent of spices that floated in the air. Chinese lanterns lit up the corners.

Jack guided her toward what he claimed

was his favorite restaurant, his hand holding hers. Lacey enjoyed being linked with him, so much so that she was almost frightened by the sense of rightness she experienced.

When they approached a steep flight of stairs that looked like something the Maya had constructed deep in the interior of Mexico, Lacey balked.

"It isn't as bad as it looks." Jack placed an arm around her waist. Lacey could deal with the stairs far easier than she could this newfound intimacy. It didn't help that she'd been up and down three flights several times that day. She explained what had happened with the office elevator, and Jack was appropriately sympathetic.

Dinner started with hot and sour soup, followed by pot stickers in hot oil. Jack did the ordering, insisting she try Szechuan chicken, prawns with chili sauce, and hot pepper beef. Every now and again he'd look at her to be sure she approved of his choices.

"We'll never eat all that," she insisted, leaning toward him until her stomach was pressed against the side of the linen-covered table.

"I know," he said, unconcerned. "There'll be plenty of leftovers for later."

It amazed her that they had so much to talk about. He respected her privacy and didn't pry into subjects she didn't want to discuss. He listened and his laugh was easy, and before she knew it she was completely relaxed. Her problems seemed much less important.

Lacey even managed to sample each of the multiple dishes Jack ordered, none of which she'd tasted before. They were so good, it was hard to stop eating.

By the time they left the restaurant, carrying the leftovers, Lacey was full and content. They walked along the crowded streets, stopping now and again to investigate the wares of a souvenir shop. Jack bought her a bar of jasmine-scented soap and a catnip toy for Cleo.

"Tell her it's from Dog," he said.

She smiled up at him. "I will. It's the least he can do."

"The very least," Jack agreed.

She had trouble pulling her gaze away from his. It had been a long time since she'd had such a happy time with a man.

"We'd better head back," Jack said abruptly, waving to flag down a taxi.

"So soon?" she protested, not understanding the swift change in his mood. One moment they were enjoying each other's company, and the next Jack looked as if he couldn't get home fast enough. He turned and looked at her, his eyes burning into hers. "I don't want to leave either."

"Then why are we going?"

"Because I can't go another minute without kissing you, and doing it on the streets of Chinatown might embarrass you."

Five

NEITHER SPOKE ON THE RIDE BACK TO THE apartment building. Jack paid the driver, took hold of Lacey's hand, and led her into the lobby. The elevator was waiting with the door wide open, and the instant they were inside Jack reached for her.

The moment their lips met, Lacey realized she'd been half crazy with wanting him. His mouth was firm and needy, as needy as her own. Standing on the tips of her toes, she linked her arms around his neck.

When he lifted his mouth from hers, she buried her face in his shoulder. He held her close, rubbing his chin across the crown of her head. His touch was as gentle as she knew it would be. Cleo trusted this touch, savored it. Now it was her turn.

She wanted him to kiss her again, needed

him to, so she'd know this was real. Reading her mind, he used his thumb to raise her chin. His eyes met and held her for a breath-stopping moment before he lowered his lips to hers. His mouth was wet and warm, coaxing. Lacey sighed as her emotions churned like the dense fog that swirls around the Golden Gate Bridge.

This was real, she decided. It didn't get any more real than this. One moment she was clinging to him, breathless with wonder, and the next she was battling tears.

"Lacey."

She didn't answer, but freed herself enough to push the button to their floor, to escape as quickly as possible. She didn't want to talk, to explain emotions she didn't understand herself. Shaking from the impact of his touch, she realized how terribly frightened she was.

After Peter had left, she'd been in shock. If she'd examined her pain then, she would have had to acknowledge how deeply he'd wounded her.

Now there was Jack, patient, gentle Jack, who evoked a wealth of sensation. But she couldn't accept this promise of joy without first dealing with the dull, throbbing pain of her past.

"Lacey," he whispered, keeping his arms loosely wrapped around her waist. "Can you tell me what's wrong?"

She shook her head. An explanation was beyond her. "I'm fine." It was a small white lie. She hadn't been fine from the moment she'd learned that Peter was involved with another woman. She felt broken and inadequate. She had never recovered from the crippling loss of the dream she'd carried with her since she was a child, playing love and marriage with paper dolls.

It wasn't supposed to happen like this. Marriage was forever. Love was supposed to last longer than a night, commitment longer than a few months.

All that Lacey had gotten out of her years with Peter was a bitterness buried so deep in her soul that it took the tenderness of another man, one she barely knew, to make her realize what she'd been doing for the past eighteen months.

Silently, Jack walked with her down the hall that led to her apartment. Pausing outside her door, he brushed a tendril of hair from her face, his touch light and nonthreatening.

"Thank you," he whispered, gently pressing his lips to hers.

She blinked. Twice. "Why are you thanking me?"

A smile lifted the edges of his mouth. "You'll know soon enough."

Her hand trembled when she inserted the key. Cleo was there to greet her, clearly unhappy at having been left so long. It took several moments for Lacey to pull herself away from her thoughts.

Setting her purse aside, she wandered into the kitchen. She could hear Jack's movements on the other side, storing the leftovers in the refrigerator. She poured herself a glass of water and smiled when she heard a light tapping sound coming from the wall.

She reached over and knocked back, smiling at their silly game.

"Good night, Lacey," she heard him say.

"Good night, Jack," she whispered, and pressed her flattened palm against the wall, needing this small connection with him, yet fearing it. She was glad he couldn't see what she had done.

❁　❁　❁

LACEY COULDN'T HAVE BEEN MORE SURPRISED WHEN Sarah Walker entered Sullivan's Decorating two days after her dinner date with Jack.

"Sarah, hello!" Lacey said, standing to greet Jack's sister.

"I hope you don't mind my stopping in unexpectedly like this." Sarah glanced nervously around the crowded shop. Every available bit of space was taken up by sample books, swatches of material, and catalogs.

"Of course not."

"I was wondering if we could meet for lunch one afternoon and talk?"

Lacey was pleased, although surprised. "I'd enjoy that very much."

They agreed on a time the following week, and Sarah chose a seafood restaurant on Fisherman's Wharf, one of Lacey's all-time favorites.

Lacey saw Jack almost every evening that week, never for very long. He had a long list of convenient excuses for dropping in unannounced, easing his way into her life bit by bit. Lacey knew what he was doing, but she didn't mind. He made no attempt to kiss her again and she was grateful, but she didn't expect his patience to last much longer.

"I was divorced over a year ago," she mentioned casually one evening, not looking at him. With Cleo in her lap, Lacey felt secure enough to touch upon the truth.

Jack sat composed and relaxed on her love seat, holding a mug of coffee, his ankle resting on his knee. "I guessed as much," he said. "Do you want to talk about it?"

"Not now. Do you mind?"

It took him awhile to answer; it seemed like the longest moment of Lacey's life. "No, but I do feel we should. Someday. The sooner the better."

She knew he was right. For the past few days, she had been rewriting her journal. It was the only way she had of sorting out her feelings. The habit of keeping a record of events in her life had started while she was still in school, and for years she had written a paragraph or two at the end of each day.

After Jack kissed her, she'd gone back to the daily journal she'd kept through those painful months before her divorce. What amazed her was the lack of emotion in those brief entries. It was as if she had jotted down the details of a police report. Just the facts, nothing more. Bits and pieces of useless information while her world blew up in her face.

She'd reread one day at a time, and then with raw courage she rewrote those trauma-filled weeks, reliving each day, refusing to dull the pain. What surprised her was the incredible amount of anger she experienced. Toward Peter. And toward Michelle, the woman he'd left her to marry.

The bitterness spilled out of her pen until her hand ached and her fingers throbbed, but still she couldn't stop. It was as if the pen insisted she get it all down as quickly as possible because only then would she be well, only then could she move forward with her life.

She was afraid she was going to explode. Even Cleo knew not to come near her. Holding a box of tissues, she'd weep and pace and weep some more. Then she'd wipe her eyes, blow her nose, and toss the damp tissue willy-nilly. In the morning, she discovered a trail that reached to every room of her apartment.

Sleep avoided her. It wasn't fair. She'd purged her soul, or so she thought. Yet it was well after midnight before she'd fall into a fitful sleep.

Lacey wasn't in the mood for company the next evening when Jack arrived, but she was pleased he'd stopped by. He was easy to be with, undemanding and supportive.

Cleo jumped down from her position in Lacey's lap and strolled into the bedroom, as if she hadn't a care in the world. When Cleo left, Jack stood and moved to Lacey. He stretched out his hand to her.

She looked up at him and blinked and then, without question, gave him her hand. He clasped it firmly in his own and then lifted her from her chair. Deftly he switched position, claiming her seat, and drew her into his lap.

"You look tired." His gaze was warm and concerned.

"I'm exhausted." As well she should be after the restless night she'd spent. No matter how hard she tried, she couldn't bury the past. It prickled her like stinging nettles.

He eased her head down to his shoulder. "Are you able to talk about your marriage yet?"

It took several moments for Lacey to answer, and when she did she found herself battling back tears. "He fell in love with someone else. He'd been having an affair for months. Oh, Jack, how could I have been so stupid not to have known, not to have realized what was happening? I was so blind, so incredibly naive."

Jack's hand was in her hair. "He was a fool, Lacey. You realize that, don't you?"

"I . . . all I know is that Peter's happy and I'm miserable. It isn't fair. I want to make him hurt the way he hurt me." She buried her face in his chest.

When her sobs subsided, Lacey realized Jack was making soft, comforting sounds. Wiping the moisture from her face, she raised her head and attempted a smile.

"Did you understand anything I said?"

"I heard your pain, and that was enough."

Appreciation filled her. She didn't know how to tell him all that was in her heart. How grateful she was for his friendship, for showing her that she'd anesthetized her life, blocked out any chance of another relationship. Little by little, he'd worn down her resistance. All she could think to do was thank him with a kiss.

It had been so very long since a man had held her like this. It had been ages since anyone had stirred up the fire deep within her. Their mouths met, shyly at first, then gaining in intensity. After only a few seconds, Lacey was drowning in a wealth of sensation.

A frightening kind of excitement took hold of her. It had been like this when Jack had kissed her that first time, but even more so now. She opened to him and sighed with surprise and delight as his hold around her tightened. Her initial response was shy.

"Lacey," he groaned, "do you have any idea how much you tempt me?"

"I do?" She basked in the glow of his words. After Peter, she'd been convinced no man would ever find her desirable again.

"We have to stop now."

Lacey had never meant for their kissing to develop to this point, but now that it had, she had few regrets. "Thank you," she whispered and lightly kissed his lips as she refastened her blouse.

"You didn't tell me very much about your divorce," he said.

"But I did," she assured him. "I told you almost everything."

He frowned. "Was I a good listener?"

"The very best," she said, with a warm

smile. "You made me feel desirable when I was convinced no man would ever want me again."

Jack closed his eyes as if attempting to fathom such a thing. "He must have been crazy."

"I . . . can't answer that."

"Do you still hate him?"

She lowered her eyes, not wanting him to read what was going on inside her. She had thought she did. Now she wasn't so sure. "I don't know. For a long time, I pretended the divorce didn't matter. I told myself I was lucky to have learned the kind of husband he was before we had children.

"It's only been since I met you that I realized how deeply I'd buried myself in denial. The divorce hurt, Jack. It was the most painful experience of my life." She wrapped her arms around his neck. "Every time I think about Peter, I feel incredibly sad."

"That's a beginning," Jack said softly, rubbing his chin against the side of her face. "A very good beginning."

Six

I'M SO PLEASED WE COULD MEET," SARAH SAID when Lacey arrived at the seafood restaurant. Seagulls flew overhead, chasing crows. The crows retaliated, pursuing the gulls in a battle over fertile feeding territory. From their window seat, Lacey could watch a lazy harbor seal sunning himself on the long pier. The day was glorious, and she felt the beginnings of joy creep into her soul. It had been a long, dark period. Her life had been dry and barren since the day Peter announced he wanted a divorce.

"I wanted to talk to you about Jack," Sarah said, her gaze fixed on her menu.

This didn't surprise Lacey, and if the truth be known she'd agreed to have lunch with Sarah for the same reason. Her curiosity about Jack was keen. He was an attractive, successful banker. They were about the same age, she guessed, and she couldn't help wondering how he'd gotten to the ripe old age of thirty-three without being married.

"I understand you and Jack are seeing each other quite a bit these days."

Lacey didn't know why the truth unsettled her so, but she found herself fiddling with her napkin, bunching it in her hands. "He comes over to visit Cleo."

Sarah's soft laugh revealed her amusement. "It isn't Cleo who interests him, and we both know it. He's had his eye on you for over a year. The problem is, my dear brother doesn't know how to be subtle."

Lacey disagreed. "He's been more than patient."

"True," Sarah agreed reluctantly. "He didn't want to scare you off. We talked about you several times. He wanted my advice. I was the one who suggested he send you flowers. He was downright discouraged when you repeatedly turned him down. Who would have thought that silly tomcat would be the thing to bring you two together?"

Lacey smoothed the linen napkin across

her lap. The time for being coy had long since passed. "I like your brother very much."

"He's wonderful." Once again Sarah admitted this with reluctance. "He liked you from the moment he first saw you."

"But why?" When Lacey moved into the apartment building she'd been an emotional wreck. The divorce had been less than a month old. She hadn't realized it at the time, but she'd been one of the walking wounded.

Sarah's look was knowing. "Jack's like that. He knew you'd been badly hurt and that you needed someone, the same way Dog did. He found Dog in a back alley, half starved and so mad he wouldn't let anyone near him. It took several weeks before Dog recognized Jack as a friend." She paused, leaned forward, and braced her elbows against the table. "But Jack was patient. He's been patient with you too, and it's paid off. I can't remember the last time he was so happy."

"I'm not a stray cat," Lacey said defensively. She wasn't keen on the comparison, but the similarity didn't escape her.

"Oh, no," Sarah said quickly. "I didn't mean

to imply that. Jack would have my head for even suggesting such a thing. But you were hurting and Jack recognized it. If you want the truth, I think Jack should have been a doctor. It's just part of his nature to want to help others."

"I see." Lacey wasn't finding this conversation the least bit complimentary, but she couldn't deny what Sarah said. For the last year she'd been walking around in a shell. Only when Jack came into her life did she understand how important it was to deal with her divorce.

Sarah sighed and set the menu aside. "Jack's wonderful. That's why it's hard to understand why he's so unreasonable about me and Mark."

"I've never known Jack to be unreasonable."

"But he is," Sarah said, keeping her head lowered as if she was close to tears. "I love Mark; we want to be married someday. We just can't marry now, for a number of reasons. Sometimes I think Jack hates him."

"I'm sure that's not true." Lacey couldn't imagine Jack hating anyone, but she could easily understand his being overprotective.

"It's true," Sarah said heatedly. "Jack refuses to have anything to do with Mark, and do you know why?" Lacey wasn't given the opportunity to answer. "Because Jack thinks Mark's using me. Nothing I can say will convince him otherwise. It's the most ridiculous thing I've ever heard, and it's all because we're living together. As far as I can see, my brother needs to wake up and smell the coffee."

The waiter arrived with glasses of ice water and a basket filled with warm sourdough bread. Lacey smiled her appreciation, grateful for the interruption. The aroma of fresh bread was heavenly, but the conversation was becoming uncomfortable. She was not sure how to reply to Sarah. She was far more at ease having Sarah answer her questions about Jack than playing go-between for brother and sister. Jack might be overprotective, but she couldn't imagine his disliking Mark without cause.

"What I'd really like is for you to talk to Jack for me," Sarah said, her eyes wide and pleading. "He'll listen to you, because—"

"I can't do that, Sarah," Lacey interrupted.

"I was hoping you'd consider it. I thought if you met Mark yourself, you'd be able to see how marvelous he is, and then you could tell Jack. You don't mind if he joins us, do you?"

Once again, Lacey wasn't given an opportunity to choose one way or the other. Sarah half rose from her seat and waved.

A sophisticated young man moved away from the bar and walked toward them, carrying his drink. Lacey studied Mark, trying to keep an open mind. As far as looks went, he was an attractive man. He kissed Sarah's cheek, but his gaze moved smoothly to Lacey and lingered approvingly. They exchanged brief handshakes while Sarah made the introductions.

"I hope you don't mind if I join you," Mark said, pulling out a chair, "although every man here will think I'm greedy to be dining with the two most beautiful women in the room."

Mark didn't need to say another word for Lacey to understand Jack's disapproval. He was much too smooth. And she didn't like the way he looked at her—with a little too much curiosity. What she didn't understand was how Sarah could be so blind.

"Sarah and I are in a bit of a quandary." Mark reached for Sarah's hand and gripped it in his own.

"We need help in dealing with Jack," Sarah elaborated. "Mark suggested the two of us get together and talk to you about our problem. I'm not sure it's wise, but Mark seems to think that you—"

"Right," Mark cut in. "I feel you might say something that would smooth the waters between Sarah and her brother for me."

"You want me to talk to Jack on your behalf?" she asked. Apparently Mark had no qualms about having her do his speaking for him. What Sarah's lover failed to understand was that Jack would react negatively to such an arrangement. Whatever small respect he had for Mark would be wiped out.

"Just mention that you've met Mark," Sarah coaxed. "You don't need to make an issue of it. I'm sure he'd listen to you. You see, Jack's living in the Middle Ages. Mark thinks Jack is jealous. My brother and I used to be really close—there wasn't anything I couldn't tell him." A wistful look clouded her pretty features. "It isn't like that anymore. It hurts, the way we argue. I can't help agreeing that it seems like jealousy."

Lacey wondered if that could possibly be true. "Jack's met Mark?"

"Oh, yes, plenty of times. From the very first, Jack's had a grudge against him."

"We started off on the wrong foot," Mark admitted dryly.

"What happened?" Lacey asked.

"Nothing," Sarah said defensively. "Absolutely nothing. But I've never been serious about anyone before, and Jack just can't deal with it."

Lacey didn't want to take sides, but she found herself saying, "I don't know Jack all that well, but I can't see him as the jealous sort."

"I know, but you see, I'm crazy about Mark and Jack knows it, and the way Mark figures—and me too—my brother needs to accept the fact that his little sister is all grown up, and he refuses to do it." Absently, Sarah tore off a piece of bread and held it between her hands, as if she wasn't sure what to do with it. "Can you help us, Lacey?"

"I doubt it," she said, as forthrightly and honestly as she could.

"Jack would listen to you," Sarah said.

Lacey smiled softly at the fervor of Sarah's belief that she had any influence on her brother. "I'm only his next-door neighbor."

"That's where you're wrong," she said, her voice raised with the strength of her conviction. "Jack really likes you. More than anyone in a good long while."

Lacey wasn't sure of that either, but she let it pass. "You want me to tell your brother that you're a mature woman capable of making her own decisions, whether he agrees with them or not."

"Exactly," Sarah said.

"That's what he needs to hear," Mark concurred.

"As an adult, you're free to love whomever you wish," Lacey said.

"Right again." Sarah's voice raised with the fervor of her conviction.

Mark smiled at Sarah and she smiled back. "We know what we're doing, isn't that right, baby?"

"I'm over twenty-one," Sarah announced.

"You're both competent judges of character," Lacey said.

"Of course." Sarah's grin widened. "I couldn't have said it better myself."

They were momentarily interrupted by the waiter, who returned for their order.

"Jack's not an unreasonable person," Lacey continued. "If that's the way you both feel, you don't need me to tell him. Do it yourselves, together."

"He won't listen," Sarah protested.

"Have you tried?"

Mark tore the roll in half and lowered his gaze. "Not exactly, but then it isn't like we've had much of an opportunity."

"Is it your living arrangement that's troubling Jack?" Lacey asked.

"That isn't permanent," Sarah told her.

"We'll be married someday," Mark said. "But not right away. We want to be married on our terms and not have them dictated by an older brother."

Lacey kept silent because she feared her own views on the subject wouldn't be welcome. Over the years several of her friends had opted for live-in arrangements. It might have been the luck of the draw, but they'd all come out of the relationships with regrets.

"Loving Mark isn't a mistake," Sarah insisted a bit too strongly. "We're perfect together."

The waiter delivered their salads, but by then Lacey had lost her appetite.

"And Sarah's perfect for me," Mark added, before reaching for his fork and digging into the plump shrimp that decorated the top of his huge salad.

"Mark loves me, and I love him," Sarah concluded. "As far as I'm concerned that's the most important thing."

Lacey saw that both Sarah and Mark felt they could change her mind. It was important to clear that up immediately. "I hope you can appreciate why I can't speak to Jack on your behalf."

"Yes," Sarah said sadly. "I just wish Jack wasn't so openly hostile."

"Sarah?" The husky male voice came from behind her. "Lacey? What are you two doing here?"

It was Jack.

Seven

HELLO, JACK," SARAH SAID, RECOVERING first. She didn't look pleased. Lacey knew their relationship was strained and wished she could help, but she couldn't think of a way to lessen the tension between them. Jack ignored Mark completely. But then Mark didn't acknowledge him either.

"How are my two best girls?" Jack asked, disregarding Sarah's cool welcome. He slid out a chair and sat down without waiting for an invitation.

"Feel free to join us," Sarah muttered sarcastically.

"Hello, Jack," Lacey said, her heart reacting in a happy way despite Sarah and Mark's sour reception. She lowered her gaze abruptly when he focused his eyes on her. She didn't have any reason to feel guilty, but she did—a little. It wasn't like she was doing something behind his back.

"Lacey and I were just having a little chat," Sarah said, after an awkward moment. "That's what you want to know, isn't it?"

"I didn't ask, Sarah. What you and Lacey talk about is none of my business." Jack ordered a cup of coffee and turned toward Lacey and Sarah, presenting Mark with a view of his back.

"If you must know, we discussed Mark and me," Sarah said, far more defensively than necessary.

Jack sipped his coffee, giving no outward indication that the topic of conversation troubled him. "Let's change the subject, shall we?"

"I bet you were hoping Lacey would talk some sense into me," Sarah said stiffly. "Well, you're wrong."

Jack leveled his gaze on his sister, his look wide and disapproving.

"You don't need to worry," Sarah continued on the same touchy note. "Lacey has refused to talk to you on our behalf."

"Mark asked her to?"

"Of course," Sarah returned belligerently.

"What else can he do since you flatly refuse to speak to him?"

"I don't appreciate your dragging Lacey into this," Jack said, not bothering to hide his disapproval.

"You don't need to worry," Sarah snapped back. "It won't happen again."

It upset Lacey to watch the two of them bicker, knowing how deeply they cared for each other. But she was helpless to do anything more than listen.

"How's Cleo?" Jack looked at Lacey in a clear effort to find a more pleasant topic.

Lacey reached for her coffee. "Getting fat."

"Good," he said absently.

"How can you ignore Mark like this?" Sarah demanded. "You act as if he isn't even here."

Jack remained stubbornly silent for a moment before asking, "Have you ever asked Mark why I behave toward him the way I do?" He sipped his coffee. "It would be very interesting if he admitted the truth."

"Let's get out of here." Mark stood abruptly and reached for Sarah's hand. "We don't need him, Sarah, we never have. Let's just leave well enough alone."

"But, Mark—" Sarah looked from her lover to her brother, her eyes bright with indecision.

"Are you coming or not?" Mark demanded irritably, dropping her hand.

"You could try talking to Jack," Sarah suggested on a tentative note, sounding unsure and pitiful. Lacey's heart went out to her.

"Do what you want." Mark turned and started to walk away.

Sarah vacillated, torn with indecision, before sighing heavily. "Mark, wait," she called, obediently trotting after him.

The silence that followed Sarah's departure was heavy with tension. Jack's face darkened with what appeared to be regret before he looked once more to Lacey. It seemed, for an awkward moment, that he had forgotten she was there.

"Jack," she said softly, touching his hand.

"I'm sorry." He shook his head as if to clear it. "I hope Sarah and Mark didn't make pests of themselves."

"Not in the least," Lacey assured him. "She's a delightful young woman, if a bit confused." Although it wasn't any of Lacey's business, she wanted to know. "Why do you actively dislike Mark?"

"There are several reasons," he said pointedly, "but you don't need to worry about me and my sister. It's not your affair."

"I see," she answered. She couldn't help feeling hurt by his abrupt dismissal. "I shouldn't have asked."

Jack sighed. "I saw him with another girl soon after Sarah moved in with him. It was clear they were more than casual acquaintances, but when I mentioned it to Sarah she claimed I was lying in an effort to break them up. Naturally Mark denied everything. It's like my beautiful, intelligent sister has been hypnotized. She can't seem to see what's right under her nose."

"It's probably the most difficult thing you can do, isn't it?"

"What?" Jack wanted to know.

Lacey gently squeezed his hand. "Watch her make a mistake and know there's no way to keep her from making it."

Jack studied her for a long moment and nodded. "It's hell. And the worst part is losing the closeness we once shared. I don't know how she can be so blind."

"Sarah can't see what she doesn't want to see." It had been the same way with Lacey. The evidence was there, but she'd refused to notice what was apparent to everyone else.

❖   ❖   ❖

WHEN LACEY RETURNED TO THE OFFICE, HER HEAD was filled with Jack and his sister. She wished there were some way she could help but knew it was impossible.

Mr. Sullivan was waiting for her, impatiently pacing the cramped quarters. As she stepped inside, he glanced pointedly at his watch.

"You're late," he announced.

"Five minutes," she said calmly, sitting down at her desk. After all the times she'd come in early and stayed late, she certainly didn't feel guilty for going five minutes over her lunch hour.

"Were you aware Mrs. Baxter was due this afternoon to go over wallpaper samples?" he asked, with thinly disguised irritation.

"Yes," Lacey answered, not understanding why her employer was so flustered.

"Well, Mrs. Baxter was in town earlier than she anticipated and stopped in. You weren't here." Accusation rang in his voice as clear as church bells. "I was left to deal with her myself, and I don't mind telling you, Lacey, that woman unnerves me. You should have been here."

Lacey straightened in her chair, unwilling to accept his censure. "Mr. Sullivan," she said evenly, refusing to allow him to badger her, "I'm entitled to my lunch hour."

He pressed his lips together and walked over to his own desk. "You're the wallpaper expert," he returned flippantly.

"I am?" If he felt that way, he should pay her accordingly. There would never be a better time to point this out.

"Of course you are," he snapped. "Whenever customers are interested in wallpaper I refer them to you."

"How nice," Lacey said.

He was making this almost easy for her. To her surprise, she wasn't the least bit nervous.

"How long have I worked for you now, Mr. Sullivan?"

"Ah . . ." He picked up a pencil and figured some numbers on a pad as if her question required several algebraic calculations. "It must be a year or more."

"Exactly a year. Do you recall that when you hired me we made an agreement?"

"Yes, of course." He stiffened as if he knew what was coming.

"There was to be a salary evaluation after six months and another at one year. The months have slipped by, and I've taken on a good deal of the responsibility of running the business for you, and now you tell me I'm your wallpaper expert! I can assure you no *expert* makes the low wages I do. I believe, Mr. Sullivan, that you owe me a substantial raise, possibly two." Having said all this in one giant breath, she was winded when she finished.

She'd done it! After all the weeks of moaning and groaning, of complaining and berating herself, she'd actually asked for the raise she deserved. It hadn't even been hard! She watched her employer and waited for his response.

"I owe you a raise?" Mr. Sullivan sounded shocked, as if the thought had never occurred to him. "I'll have to check my records. You might very well be right. I'll look into it and get back to you first thing in the morning." Having

said that, Mr. Sullivan promptly disappeared—
something he was doing more frequently of
late, leaving her with the burden of dealing
with everything herself.

Lacey felt as though a great weight had been
lifted from her shoulders. It was as if whatever
had bound her had fallen away.

❖ ❖ ❖

THE FIRST PERSON SHE SOUGHT OUT THAT AFTERNOON
was Jack. She went directly from the elevator to
his apartment, knocking several times, eager
to share her news. To her disappointment, he
wasn't home. She realized how important he'd
become to her. It was as if none of this were real
until she'd shared it with her neighbor.

Letting herself inside her own apartment,
she promptly greeted Cleo and then reached
for the phone. Jeanne answered on the second
ring.

"I asked Mr. Sullivan for a raise," she said
without so much as a hello. "Jeanne, I'm so
happy, I could cry. It just happened. He made
some offhand comment about me being his
wallpaper expert, and I said if that was the case
I should be properly compensated."

"That's great, and about time too, girl. Congratulations!"

Lacey knew Jeanne would be pleased for
her, if for nothing more than garnering the
courage to ask.

"I owe you so much," Lacey said, the emotion bubbling in her voice. "I really do. Not long
ago you claimed if I wanted to be a victim, you
couldn't help me, and I realized you were right.
And Jack too, he's been—" She stopped, thinking how much Jack had helped her. Not in the
same way as Jeanne, but by his own gentle understanding, he'd encouraged her and helped
her to find herself. She understood for the first
time how confronting Mr. Sullivan was tied in
with her divorce. She'd come out of her marriage emotionally crippled, carrying a load of
grief and insecurity that had burdened her
whole life.

"You haven't mentioned Jack much lately,"
Jeanne commented. "How's it going with you
two?"

"I haven't talked about Jack?" Lacey
hedged. "It's going fine, just fine."

"*Fine* suggests it's going great."

Cleo wove her way around Lacey's feet, demanding attention. With the tip of her shoe, Lacey booted the catnip toy as a distraction. Cleo raced after it.

"Now," Jeanne said, heaving a giant breath, "tell me how much of a raise Mr. Sullivan's giving you."

"He didn't say . . . exactly. All he said was that he was going to think about it overnight."

"Don't let him weasel out of it," Jeanne warned.

"Don't worry," Lacey said. "He wouldn't dare." At the moment she felt invincible, capable of dealing with anything or anyone.

As soon as she was off the phone, Lacey gave Cleo the attention she demanded. "How are you doing, girl?" Lacey asked. "I bet you're anxious to have those kittens." She stroked her back and Cleo purred contentedly. "Jack and I will find good homes for your babies," Lacey assured her. "You don't have a thing to worry about."

Jack didn't get home until after six. The minute she heard movement on the other side of her kitchen wall, she hurried over to his apartment. She tapped out a staccato knock against his door and was cheered to hear him humming on the other side.

"Who is it?" he called out.

"Lacey."

The door flew open. The minute he appeared, she vaulted into his arms, spreading kisses over his face. He blinked as if he wasn't sure what was happening.

"Lacey?" His eyes were wide with surprise and delight. "What was that for?"

"A thank-you." She wove her arms around his neck and kissed him again. "I'm so happy."

"My guess is something happened after we met at lunch."

She rewarded his genius, taking more time, savoring the kiss. With every beat of her heart, she thanked God for sending Jack into her lonely, bleak life.

"I'm almost afraid to ask what this is all about. Whatever it is, don't let me stop you." He closed the door with his foot and carried her into the living room.

She hugged him tight. His shirt was unfastened. Either he was dressing or undressing, she couldn't tell which. Her trembling body moved against his.

"Are you going to tell me what we're celebrating?" he asked her breathlessly.

"A raise," she said. "And long overdue. You see, I had to ask for it, and doing that was a growing experience for me." She paused to rub her nose against his. "I realize this probably sounds silly, but I couldn't make myself ask, and it got to be this really big thing, like a monster, and then I was terrified."

"But you did it?"

"Yes. I owe it all to you—and to my friend Jeanne. Knowing you has helped me so much, Jack. You've given me my confidence back. I'm not sure how you managed it, but since we've been . . . neighborly, it seems everything's turned around for me."

"I couldn't be more pleased, and naturally I'll accept the credit," he said warmly.

"Mr. Sullivan's going to think about it overnight, but you see this isn't about the money. It's about me."

"You certainly didn't have any problem confronting me when Dog stole Cleo's virginity. As I recall you were ready with a tidy list of demands."

"That was different. I wasn't the one affected, it was Cleo. I didn't have the least bit of trouble sticking up for my cat."

"I'd like to complain, but I won't," Jack said. "I'm more than pleased that Dog decided to call upon Cleo; otherwise I don't know how long it would have taken me to break through those barriers of yours."

He kissed her then, slowly, thoroughly, leaving her trembling when he'd finished.

"We'll celebrate. Dinner, dancing, a night on the town. We'll—" He stopped abruptly and closed his eyes.

"What?"

"I've got another one of those stupid dinner meetings this evening."

"It doesn't matter." She was disappointed, but she understood. "This is rather short notice. We'll celebrate another time. It doesn't matter, truly it doesn't." Nothing could mar her happiness. "How soon do you have to leave?"

He glanced at his watch and frowned. "Ten minutes."

"I'd better go."

"No." He kissed her hungrily.

"Jack"—she managed a protest, weak at best—"you'll be late for your dinner."

"Yeah, I know."

"Jack!"

He kissed her nose. "Spoilsport. Remember, we're on for dinner on the town tomorrow night."

"I'll remember."

Lacey returned to her apartment in a daze. When she slumped onto the sofa, Cleo settled in her lap, and she slowly stroked the cat's back, thinking over her day. Lacey wasn't sure how long she sat there before someone knocked on her door. Checking the peephole, Lacey was shocked to see who it was.

"Sarah!" she said, unlocking her door.

Jack's sister took one look at her and burst into tears. "Oh, Lacey, I've been such a fool!"

Eight

SARAH, WHAT HAPPENED?" LACEY LED JACK'S sister into her apartment. Sarah slumped onto the love seat and covered her face with both hands. Several seconds passed before she was able to speak.

"I . . . found out Mark's involved with someone else. I found them together, in our bed. I thought I was going to be sick . . . I couldn't believe my own eyes. How could I have been so stupid?"

"Oh, Sarah!" Lacey wrapped her arm around Sarah's shoulders. "I'm so sorry."

"Jack *told* me Mark was seeing someone else, but I didn't believe him. I loved Mark . . . I really loved him. How could I have been so stupid?" She buried her face in Lacey's shoulder.

The experience was nearly a mirror image

of her own, so Lacey could appreciate the devastating sense of betrayal Sarah was feeling.

"I know what you're going through," Lacey said when Sarah's sobbing had slowed. She brought her a hot cup of tea with plenty of sugar to help ward off the shock.

"How could you?" Sarah said. She looked up at Lacey, her face devoid of makeup, her eyes filled with a hollow, familiar pain. The afghan Lacey's mother had crocheted for a Christmas present was wrapped over the younger woman's shoulders as if she'd been chilled to the bone. Sarah looked as if she were six years old.

"It's like your whole world has been violently turned upside down. But it's much more than that. The sense of betrayal is the worst emotional pain there is."

"You too?"

Lacey nodded. "My husband—ex-husband, now—left me for another woman. Apparently they'd been lovers for months, but I didn't have a clue. When Peter asked for a divorce, I thought I'd die." Memories of that final confrontation filtered through Lacey's mind. She found, somewhat to her surprise, that although they saddened her, she didn't feel the crushing agony that had been with her for the last year and a half.

"What . . . what did you do afterward?"

Lacey reached for Sarah's hand and squeezed her fingers. "After the divorce was final, I packed everything I owned and moved to San Francisco."

"Then it must not have been very long ago."

"The divorce was final last year about this time."

Sarah sipped her tea. "I was blind to what was happening. I trusted Mark, really trusted him. I nearly allowed him to destroy my love for my brother."

"Don't blame yourself."

"But I do!" Sarah cried. "Looking back, I can't believe I sided against Jack. He's never lied to me, and yet I believed everything Mark was telling me about my brother being jealous and all that other garbage."

"I believed too," Lacey said, "but when you love someone, the trust is automatic. Why should we suspect a man of cheating when such behavior would never occur to us? The very thought of being unfaithful to Peter was repugnant to me."

Sarah cradled the mug between her palms. "Do you think you'll ever be able to trust a man again?"

"Yes," Lacey answered, after some length, "but not in the same blind way. I couldn't bear to live my life being constantly suspicious. The burden of that would ruin any future relationships. I'm not the same woman I was eighteen months ago. Peter's betrayal has marked me forever." She hesitated, unsure of how much she should admit about the changes knowing Jack had brought into her life. "It wasn't until recently that I felt I could say this, but I believe it changed me for the better."

"How do you mean?"

"It was a long, painful ordeal. Only in the last month have I come to terms with what happened. For a long time I thought I hated Peter, but that wasn't true. How could I hate him when I'd never stopped loving him?"

"What do you feel for him now?"

Lacey had to think over the question. "Mostly I don't feel anything. I've forgiven him."

"You? He should be the one to beg *your* forgiveness."

Lacey smiled, knowing Peter as she did.

"I could wait until hell freezes over, and that would never happen. Peter believes *I* was the one who failed *him*, and perhaps I did in some way. He needed an excuse to rationalize what he was doing."

"Mark blamed me too. How could you forgive Peter? I don't understand."

"You'd be right to say he didn't ask for my forgiveness. But I didn't do it for *him*, I did it for *me*. Otherwise his betrayal would have destroyed me."

"I still don't understand."

"In the beginning," Lacey said, "I couldn't deal with the pain so I pretended I wasn't hurt. But in the last month, I've realized that I needed to let go of Peter and the failed marriage, and the only way to do it was to admit my own faults and forgive him. If I didn't, I might never have let go of my bitterness."

Fresh tears brimmed in Sarah's eyes. "I'll never be as wise as you are."

Lacey laughed. "Oh, Sarah, if only you knew how very long it took me to reconcile myself to this divorce. I have Jack to thank, and my friend Jeanne. Even Cleo played a role."

"Jack's wonderful," Sarah admitted and bit

her lower lip. "I've treated him abominably."

"That's one thing about brothers, they're forgiving. At least we can trust that Jack is. He's a special man, Sarah, and I can't believe you'll have any more problems setting matters straight with him."

They sat and talked, and as the hours passed Lacey realized how much they had in common. It was nearly ten o'clock when the doorbell chimed. The two women looked at each other.

"You don't need to worry. I'm sure it's not Mark."

Lacey checked the peephole anyway. It was Jack. Unlatching the chain, she opened the door and was immediately brought into his arms. He kissed her as if it had been weeks instead of hours since they'd last seen each other.

"Jack." Sarah's voice cut into the sensual fog that surrounded Lacey.

Jack abruptly broke off the kiss but kept his arm around Lacey's waist. She watched his face as he discovered his sister sitting on the sofa, wrapped in Lacey's afghan. His gaze went from Sarah to Lacey and then back again.

"Sit down," Lacey said, easing her way out

of his embrace. "Sarah has something to tell you." Then, because she knew how difficult it would be, she leaned close and whispered, "Be gentle with her."

❖   ❖   ❖

"LACEY," JACK SAID IRRITABLY, "DON'T LIFT THAT, it's too heavy for you."

"I'm fine," she insisted, hauling the carton out of the back of the rented van. It was heavy, but nothing she couldn't handle. Sarah had found an apartment of her own, and Jack and Lacey were helping her move. It had been an eventful month. Sarah had temporarily moved in with Lacey and the two women had talked, often long into the night.

"That should do it," Sarah said, as Lacey set the carton on the kitchen countertop. She looked past Lacey and whispered, "What's wrong with Jack? He's been a real crab all morning, and he wasn't much better last night, either. Did you notice?"

Lacey had, but she hadn't wanted to say anything. "I don't know what's wrong." But something was.

"If anyone can get it out of him, it's you."

Lacey wondered if that was true. After the last month she felt as close to Sarah as if they were really sisters. And in that time she'd come to another, more profound realization.

She was deeply in love with Jack.

For someone who was convinced she was constitutionally incapable of falling in love again, this was big news.

"I can't thank you two enough," Sarah said when Jack returned from the truck. "I don't know what I would have done these last weeks without you." She hugged them, then turned away in an effort to hide the tears that glistened in her dark eyes. "I'll be fine now. You two go and have fun. I don't want you to worry about me."

Jack hesitated. "You're sure?"

"Positive." Sarah made busywork around her compact kitchen, removing several items from the closest box and setting them on the counter. All the while her back was to them. "Please," she added.

Remembering her own experience, Lacey whispered, "She'll be fine. All she needs is time."

Together Lacey and Jack walked outside to where Jack had parked the moving van. He opened the passenger door and helped her inside.

Lacey removed her bandanna and shook her head to free the thick strands of dark hair that were plastered against her face. Jack climbed into the driver's seat. She noticed how his hands tightened around the steering wheel. For several seconds he just sat there. Then he started the engine and moved out into traffic. But he still seemed deep in thought. Something was wrong.

"Jack," she said softly, "what's troubling you?"

Her voice broke him out of his reverie, and he smiled as if he hadn't a care in the world. "Not a thing. How about sharing a hot fudge sundae with me after we take the truck back?"

It sounded wonderful, but Lacey had discovered in the last few weeks that almost every minute she spent in Jack's company was special. *He* was special.

"Are you worried about Sarah?" Lacey pried gently, wondering at his somber mood. Something was on his mind, but she couldn't force him to tell her. He would speak up when he was ready, she decided.

"Not as much now as when she was living with Mark. Although it's been hard on her, discovering exactly what kind of man he is was the best thing that could have happened."

"She'll be fine," Lacey said confidently.

"Thanks to you."

"Oh, hardly. Sarah will come away from this experience a little more mature and a whole lot smarter. I know I did with Peter. But it takes time. Rome wasn't built in a day."

"I'll say. Look how long it took me to get to know you."

"It was worth the effort, wasn't it?"

He took one hand from the wheel and patted her knee. They were sitting so close to each other that their hips touched. The morning was muggy, but neither of them moved, enjoying this small intimacy. "The wait was well worth the while," he agreed and then added, his eyes dark and serious, "I'm crazy about you, Lacey; I have been for months."

"I'm crazy about you too," she returned softly.

What was definitely crazy was that they should admit their feelings for each other in a moving van in the heavy flow of San Francisco traffic.

After having spoken so freely, both seemed a little embarrassed, a little relieved, and a whole lot in love. Lacey felt as if she were in college all over again. The years of her marriage and the aftermath of the divorce vanished, as if they'd never happened.

Leaving his car in the underground parking lot, they caught the elevator. The instant the door slid closed, Lacey was in Jack's arms. His mouth sought hers with the desperation of a man locked in a dark room, unable to find the exit. His arms half lifted her from the floor, giving her the perfect excuse to cling to him.

"I'm crazy about you," she said. She felt drunk, as if she'd spent the last few hours sitting in a bar instead of the last few moments in his arms.

He caught her face between his hands and kissed her until she trembled and whimpered. He moaned.

"Jack." From somewhere deep inside she managed a weak protest. "We're still in the elevator."

He lifted his head and looked around. "We are?"

She wrapped her arms around his waist and tilted back her head to smile up at him.

"Where's your sense of adventure?" he teased, kissing her nose. He reached over and pushed the button for the fourth floor.

This intense feeling of desire was new to her. If he didn't continue kissing her, loving her, touching her, Lacey thought she'd die. It was as if years of dammed-up longing had broken free deep inside of her, swamping her senses.

He kissed her again and she sagged against him just as the elevator delivered them to the fourth floor.

"Your place or mine?" he asked, and then made the decision for her. "Yours."

Her hand trembled when she gave him her keys, and she was gratified to see his fingers weren't any steadier. In that moment, she loved him so much she couldn't bear it a second longer. Her arms circled his middle and she kissed the underside of his jaw, teasing him with her tongue, running it down his neck to the hollow at the base of his throat and sucking gently.

"Lacey, stop," he protested.

"Do you mean that?" she whispered, lifting her face.

"No . . . never stop loving me." The door opened and they all but stumbled inside.

It was then she heard Cleo's pitiful meow. Jack heard it too. He glanced over his shoulder and then turned his gaze back to her. His eyes were tightly shut.

"Cleo's having her kittens," he announced and moved away from her.

Nine

"CLEO'S HAVING HER KITTENS NOW!"

Lacey hurried into the apartment.

"Oh, my goodness!" She pressed her hands over her mouth and stared into the closet, where Cleo had made herself a comfortable bed in a darkened corner.

The Abyssinian meowed pitifully.

"Oh, Cleo," Lacey whispered.

Cleo ignored her, rose from her nest, and walked over to Jack, weaving between his legs, her long tail sliding around his calf. Then moved back into the closet and cried again, softly, pleadingly.

"She seems to want you," Lacey murmured, unable to disguise her amazement. It didn't make sense that Cleo would be more comfortable with Jack. After all, Lacey was the one who fed and nurtured her.

"She wants *me*?"

"It wasn't me she was crying for just now."
Didn't anyone understand the meaning of
commitment anymore? Lacey wondered. Even
her cat turned to someone else in her moment
of need.

Cleo was up again, seeking Jack's attention.
He squatted down in front of the open closet
door and patted her gently while whispering
reassurances.

"Should I boil water or something?" Lacey
asked anxiously. The moment had finally arrived, but she hadn't a clue as to what her role
should be. She'd assumed Cleo would calmly
give birth to her kittens one day while Lacey
was at work.

"Boil water?" Jack asked. "Whatever for?"

"I . . . don't know. Coffee, I guess." She paced
the carpet behind Jack in short, quick steps.
Seconds earlier they'd been wrapped in an
impassioned embrace, and now lovemaking was
the furthest thing from either of their minds.

"How's she doing?" Lacey asked, peeking
over his shoulder.

"Great, so far. It looks as if the first kitten is
about to be born."

"How's Cleo?" Lacey asked again, her fingertips pressed against her lips. "Is she afraid? I don't think I can bear to see her in pain."

Jack looked up at Lacey, reached for her hand, and kissed her knuckles. "She's fine. Stop worrying or you'll make yourself ill."

No sooner had he said the words than Lacey's stomach cramped. She wrapped her hands around her waist, sank onto the end of the mattress, and leaned forward. "Jack, I don't feel so good."

"Go make that coffee you were talking about earlier," he suggested. "At this point Cleo's doing better than you are."

Cleo cried out and Jack turned his attention back to the closet.

"She just delivered the first kitten," he announced, his pleasure keen. "Good girl, Cleo," he said excitedly. "My goodness, will you look at that! Cleo's kitten is the spitting image of Dog."

Lacey hurried off the bed to look. Her stomach didn't feel much better, but she understood the source of her discomfort. She was experiencing sympathetic labor pains. "He does look like Dog." She squatted down next to Jack and studied the ugly little creature. "I don't mind telling you, Jack, this unnerves me."

"I could go for a cup of coffee," he said. "Cleo and I are doing fine."

Lacey hurried into the kitchen. Once she was there, she decided there was no need to rush. As Jack had so eloquently told her, he had everything under control.

"How's it going?" she asked when she returned with their coffee.

"Great. I think Cleo's just about ready to deliver a second kitten."

Lacey wasn't interested in viewing the birthing process, so she sat on the bed and let Jack play midwife.

"Here it comes," he said after a few minutes, his voice elevated with excitement. "This one's just like Dog too." He turned with a proud smile as if he'd given birth himself.

Grumbling, Lacey sank onto the carpet next to Jack. Cleo was busy licking off her tiny offspring. As far as Lacey could tell the kittens were no bigger than fur balls and ugly as sin, but that didn't keep her heart from swelling with a flood of emotions.

"Do you think she's finished?"

"I don't know," Jack returned. "How long do these things usually take?"

Lacey laughed. "How would I know?"

"You intended to breed her, didn't you?"

"Yes, before Dog so rudely interrupted my plans."

Jack wiggled his eyebrows. "You're pleased he did, aren't you?"

Lacey wasn't willing to admit anything of the sort. "You'll note that once Dog had his fun with Cleo, he was on his merry way."

"Perhaps, but with Cleo having Dog's family—well, it sort of cemented our relationship, don't you think?"

She suppressed a smile. "I guess it did."

"You can breed her next time if you're really serious about it."

He was right; it would be foolish to claim otherwise. "I'll get the pamphlet Dr. Christman gave me. That should tell us how long this process takes." She left him momentarily and returned reading the material the vet had given her.

"I think Cleo might be finished," Jack announced when Lacey walked into the bedroom and sat on the end of the mattress. "She's lavishing attention on her kittens and not acting the way she was earlier."

"It says here the birthing process generally takes a couple of hours," she recited and glanced at her watch. It hadn't taken nearly that amount of time for Cleo.

Before she could say as much, Jack said, "We don't have any idea how long she was in labor before we arrived."

"Right. It could easily have been two hours." She felt a tremendous sense of relief that it was over. "She only had two kittens, but it says right here that Abyssinians generally have smaller litters and Siamese have larger ones. That's interesting."

"I guess we should thank our lucky stars Cleo only has the two."

"Speaking of which," Lacey said righteously, "you never gave me the name of the family taking your half of the litter."

"I'll give one to Sarah," Jack said confidently. "A pet will do her good. Besides, she owes me big-time."

"But does Sarah want a cat?" Lacey might think of Jack's sister as family, but she didn't want to foist an animal off on her if Sarah wasn't willing.

"Of course she wants one. Dog and Cleo's offspring are special. Besides, a kitten will keep her company while she gets over Mark." He frowned as if he found speaking the other man's name repulsive. "It shouldn't take long for her to forget that rat."

"Don't be so sure," Lacey told him. "I was married to a man who displayed many of the same characteristics. Be patient with her," she advised again, and then added with a gentle smile, "as patient as you were with me."

"You've spoken so little of your marriage."

"If you review what happened with Sarah and change the names in the appropriate places, the story's the same, with only a few differences," she amended. "The biggest difference is that I was married to Peter. A couple of months after I moved here, I heard from a well-meaning friend who thought I should know that he'd married his blond cupcake and they were expecting a baby."

"Some friend."

Her smile was sad. "That's what I thought.

The news devastated me. Not because he'd re-married, but because he'd been adamant about us not having children when I wanted a family so badly."

Jack drank from his coffee and seemed to be mulling over the information. "You're over him now?"

Lacey wasn't entirely sure how to answer him. Her hesitation appeared to give Jack some concern. He leveled his gaze at her and frowned darkly.

"Yes, I'm over him, and no, I'm not."

The corner of Jack's mouth jerked upward. "That's about as clear as swamp water."

"I don't love him anymore, if that's what you're asking. The hardest part was having to let go of the dream of what our lives could have been like together."

"Have you?" The words were stark and issued without emotion.

"Yes." She wanted to thank him for the large part he'd played in the healing process, but he didn't seem receptive to it. Although he'd asked her about Peter and her marriage, he seemed to find it uncomfortable to listen to the sorry details of her life with her ex-husband.

Jack stood and wandered into the living room, taking his coffee with him. When she joined him, she found him standing in front of the small window that looked down over the street. He didn't turn around. It was almost as if he'd forgotten she was with him.

"Jack?"

He turned around and offered her a fleeting grin.

"Does it bother you to discuss my ex-husband?"

He shook his head, and set his mug aside. "Not in the least. I was the one who asked, remember?"

"Yes, but you seemed—I don't know, upset, I guess. Peter was a part of my life, an important part for several years.

"The divorce was difficult for me, but I learned from it. I matured. Blaming Peter isn't important any longer. I understand now that I played a part in the death of our marriage. I wasn't the perfect wife."

"You say you don't love him anymore?"

She gestured weakly. "Let me put it like this. I don't hate him. My happiness doesn't hinge on what's happening in his life. My happiness hinges on me and the choices I make, and I've decided to live a good life." She hoped it would be with Jack. With all her heart, she prayed he felt as strongly about her as she did him.

He smiled. Lacey swore she'd never seen anyone more beautiful. It was strange, she realized, to feel that way about a man. It wasn't so much his looks, although heaven knew he was handsome. What she found so appealing about Jack was who he was as a person. He was trustworthy and generous. He'd helped restore her faith in love and life. His love had been a precious gift for which she would always be thankful.

"Jack," she whispered, "what's wrong?" Something was still bothering him.

He walked over to Lacey and tenderly gathered her in his arms. He rested his chin against the top of her head, and she heard a sigh rumble through his chest.

"You got your raise from Mr. Sullivan?" he asked.

"Yes." Lacey was sure she'd told him, but they'd both been so wrapped up in helping

Sarah that he must have forgotten. "A very healthy one."

"Good."

Lacey eased away from his chest and met his gaze. "Why are you asking about Mr. Sullivan?"

"You love your job, don't you? Especially now that you're getting the respect and the money you deserve?"

"Yes, but what does that have to do with us?"

He brought her back into his embrace. "I love my job too. I've worked for California Fidelity for nearly ten years. Last Thursday I was given a promotion. This is something I've worked toward for years, but I never dreamed it would happen so quickly. It took me completely by surprise."

"Jack, that's wonderful." Stepping up on her tiptoes, she kissed him, so proud she felt she would burst. "Why didn't you say something sooner? We could have celebrated."

"My promotion means something else, Lacey."

"I'm sure you'll have added responsibilities. Oh, Jack, I couldn't be more pleased for you."

"It means," he said, cupping her shoulders, "I have to move."

The blood rushed out of her face so fast, Lacey felt faint. "Move? Where?"

He sighed and looked away from her. "Seattle."

Ten

"SEATTLE," LACEY ECHOED, STUNNED. "WHEN did you intend to tell me, before or after you had your way with me?" Stepping away from him, she pushed the hair away from her head, leaving her hands there, elbows extended. "You're no better than Dog!"

"What's Dog got to do with this? You're being ridiculous."

"I'm not. You were going to make love to me and then casually mention you were being transferred?" It was all clear to her now. Rainwater clear. Just like the tomcat he called a pet, he was going to take what he wanted and walk out of her life.

"I didn't plan anything of the sort. You don't have any reason to be so angry. Besides, nothing happened."

"Thanks to Cleo. And for your information, I . . . have every right to be angry." Her fragile voice wobbled with emotion but gained strength with each word. "It'd be best if you left."

"Not until we've talked this out." He planted his feet as if to suggest a bulldozer wouldn't budge him before he was good and ready.

She pointed her index finger at him while she gathered her thoughts together, which unfortunately had scattered like water-starved cattle toward a river. "I've heard about men like you."

"What?" He stared at her as if he needed to examine her more closely. "Lacey, for the love of heaven, stop right now before you say something you'll regret."

"I most certainly will say something." She walked over to the door and held it open for him. "You . . . you can't drop a bombshell like that and expect me not to react. As for regrets, trust me, Jack Walker, I've got plenty of those. It'll take years to sort through them all."

"All right, all right." He raised his hands in surrender. Actually he posed as if she held a six-shooter on him. "Please, close the door. Let's sit down and talk this over like two civilized people."

"Are you suggesting I'm not civilized? Because I'm telling you right now, I've had about as much as I can take."

"Sit down," he said calmly and gestured toward her sofa. "Please."

Lacey debated whether she should do as he asked or not. She crossed her arms under her breasts and glared at him. "I prefer to stand."

"Will you close the door?"

She hadn't realized her foot had continued to hold it open. "All right," she said stiffly, as if this were a large concession. Chin held high, she moved, and the door closed with a decidedly loud click.

"This is what I thought we'd do," Jack said, pacing in front of the window he'd been staring out only moments earlier.

"We?" she asked, wanting him to think she resented the way he automatically included her.

"Me," he amended, casting her a sour look. "I'm going to accept the promotion, Lacey. I thought about it long and hard, and I can't let this opportunity pass. The timing could be better, but I can't change that. I worked hard for this, and just because—"

"Of me?" she finished for him. "You don't need to worry, Jack, I wasn't going to ask you to turn down such a wonderful opportunity." Despite the shock and the betrayal she felt, maintaining her outrage was becoming difficult. Her voice softened considerably. "I wouldn't ever ask such a thing of you."

"I thought I could fly down for a weekend once a month," he suggested.

Once a month, she mused, her heart so heavy it felt as if it had dropped all the way to her knees. After having made such an issue of standing, she felt the sudden need to sit down.

Slumping onto the edge of the love seat, she bit her lower lip. So this was what was to become of them. Once-a-month dates. Lacey wasn't foolish enough to believe it would be otherwise. Long-distance relationships were difficult. They'd both start out with good intentions, but she noted he didn't say where these monthly meetings would lead.

Jack motioned with his hands. "Say something. Anything. I know it's not the ideal solution. It's going to be hard on me too."

"Expensive, too," she said. Already she could see the handwriting on the wall. He'd fly down for visits the first couple of months, and then he'd skip a month and she wouldn't hear from him the following one.

"We can make this work, Lacey."

Blinking back the tears, she stood and walked over to stand in front of him. His features blurred as her tears brimmed. She pressed her hands against the sides of his face, leaned forward, and kissed him. The electricity between them all but crackled, and it was several moments before Lacey found the strength and the courage to pull away.

"I . . . asked Sarah why you wanted to date me." She found it almost impossible to speak normally. "She told me you've been like this all your life. You find someone hurting and broken, someone in need of a little tenderness, and then you lavish them with love. What she didn't say was that once they were strong again, you'd step back and wish them a fond farewell."

Jack's brow condensed with a thick frown. "We aren't talking about the same thing. If you must know, you did represent a certain challenge from the moment we met. Until you, I'd never had much of a problem getting a woman to agree to go out with me. As for this other business, you're way off base."

"What about Dog?"

The frown darkened considerably. "What about him?"

"The lost and lonely alley cat you found and loved."

A hint of a smile touched his lips. "I don't think Dog would appreciate that description. We more or less tolerated each other in the beginning. These days, we share a tentative friendship."

"You took him in, gave him a home, and—"

"Hold on just one minute," Jack said sternly. "You're not suggesting that my friendship with Dog has anything to do with us, are you?"

It was apparent he didn't understand or appreciate the similarities. It would be one of the most difficult things she'd ever do to say goodbye to Jack, but despite what she'd claimed, she'd do it without regrets. He'd given her far more than he'd ever know. With Jack's love and support, she had learned to let go of the past. His love had given her the courage to move forward.

"Thank you," she whispered. She dropped her hands and stepped away.

"What are you thanking me for?" he demanded. "And why does it sound like another way of saying good-bye?"

She didn't so much as blink. "Because it is."

He paled visibly. "You don't mean that," he murmured.

Lacey couldn't think of anything more to say. Arguments crowded her mind. It would be easy to pretend that nothing would change after he moved to Seattle, but she knew it would.

Within a few months, Lacey would become little more than a memory of someone he once cared for. As he said, he didn't have a problem finding women interested in going out with him.

With all this talk of get-togethers, Lacey noticed, he wasn't offering her any promises. But to be fair, he hadn't sought any from her either.

"So it's over, just like that?" he said stiffly.

"It was nice knowing you, have a good life, and all that rot?"

It sounded cold and crass, but basically he had it right. Unable to look him in the eye, Lacey nodded and lowered her head.

"In other words, once I walk out that door, that's it?"

"It's better this way," she whispered, the words barely making it past the lump in her throat. She prayed he'd leave before she disgraced herself further by weeping openly.

"Easier, in the long run. I'd rather end this now and be done with it. The woman I love is ordering me out of her life. It doesn't make sense."

"Exactly what are you offering me, Jack?" she asked defiantly. "A weekend once a month . . . for how long? Two months, maybe three? It isn't going to last—"

"Why not? For your information I'm hoping it doesn't last more than a month or two myself."

His words stung as sharply as a slap across the face.

"Maybe by that time you'll be miserable enough to be willing to marry me—"

"Marry you?" Lacey wasn't sure she'd

heard him correctly, and if ever things had to be crystal clear it was now.

"Of course," he snapped. "You can't honestly believe I was planning on making this commute every month for the rest of our lives, did you?"

"Well, yes, that's exactly what I thought," she whispered.

"I figured it might take a couple of miserable months apart for you to realize you love me."

"I know I love you now, you idiot. Why else do you think I turned down a hot fudge sundae? I told you how I felt this very afternoon."

He glared at her suspiciously. "No, you didn't."

"Jack," she said impatiently, "you were driving the moving van back to the rental company, and I looked you right in the eye and said it."

"What you said was you were crazy about me. There's a world of difference between crazy and love. If you love me you're going to have to make it abundantly clear, otherwise there's going to be a problem. You already know I love you."

"No, I don't," she argued. "You've never once told me how you feel about me."

133

He shut his eyes as if he were seconds away from losing his patience. "A man doesn't say that sort of thing lightly, especially if the woman has only admitted to being crazy. Besides, you must know how I feel. A blind man on the street would know I've been in love with you from the moment you knocked on my door and demanded that Dog do right by Cleo."

"You . . . never said anything."

"How could I? You were as prickly as a cactus. It took me weeks to get you to agree to so much as a date. Just when I was beginning to think I was making some progress, along comes this promotion. What else am I supposed to do but pray you miss me so much you'll agree to marry me."

"I do," Lacey whispered.

Apparently Jack didn't hear her. "Another thing. You just got your raise, and I've never seen you so happy. You aren't going to want to uproot your life now, just when you've finally gotten what you wanted."

"I don't think you heard me, Jack. I said I do. Furthermore, if I've been happy lately, did it ever occur to you it might be because I'd fallen in love with you?"

"You do what?" he demanded impatiently.

"Agree to marry you. This minute. Tomorrow. Or two months down the road, whatever you want."

He squinted his eyes and stared at her as if he wasn't sure he should trust her. "What about your job?"

"I'll give two weeks' notice first thing in the morning."

"Your lease?"

"I'll sublet the place. Listen here, Jack Walker, if you think you're going to back down on your offer now, I've got a word or two for you."

He stood and walked all the way around her. "You're serious? You'd be willing to marry me just like that?"

Her grin widened, and she snapped her fingers. "Just like that. You don't honestly believe I'd let a wonderful man like you slip through my fingers, do you? I can't let you go, Jack." She threw her arms around his neck and spread happy, eager kisses all over his face.

Jack wrapped his arms around her waist and lifted her off the ground. Their kiss was slow, tender, and thorough. By the time they finished, Lacey was left weak and breathless.

"I'll never let you go, Jack Walker."

"That's more like it," he said with a dash of male arrogance, and pulled her tightly against him again.

It was exactly where she wanted to be. Close to his heart for all time.

HOMEMADE TREATS FOR YOUR CAT*

Cat Treats and Cat Treat Recipes

THE PET STORES ARE FULL OF CAT TREATS. BUT DID you know that you can make your own healthy kitty treats at home? Here are some recipes to help you find a way to your cat's heart.

SAVORY CHEESE TREATS

¾ cup white flour
¾ cup shredded cheddar cheese
5 tablespoons grated parmesan cheese
¼ cup plain yogurt or sour cream
¼ cup cornmeal

Preheat the oven to 350°F. Combine cheeses and yogurt. Add flour and cornmeal. If needed, add a small amount of water to create a nice

*This article has been provided courtesy of PetPlace.com (www.petplace.com), the definitive online source for pet news, health, and wellness information.

dough. Knead dough into a ball and roll to ¼ inch. Cut into 1-inch-sized pieces and place on greased cookie sheet. Bake for 25 minutes. Makes 2 dozen.

CHICK 'N' BISCUITS

1½ cups shredded cooked chicken
½ cup chicken broth
1 cup whole wheat flour
1/3 cup cornmeal
1 tablespoon soft margarine

Preheat the oven to 350°F. Combine chicken, broth, and margarine and blend well. Add flour and cornmeal. Knead dough into a ball and roll to ¼ inch. Cut into 1-inch-sized pieces and place on an ungreased cookie sheet. Bake at 350°F for 20 minutes. Makes 18 cookies.

CRISPY LIVER MORSELS

½ cup cooked chicken livers
¼ cup water
1¼ cups whole wheat flour
¼ cup cooked carrot, mashed
1 tablespoon soft margarine

Preheat the oven to 325°F. Place well-done livers in a blender with ¼ cup water. In a bowl, combine flour and margarine. Add liver mixture and carrots and knead dough into a ball. Roll dough to ¼-inch thick and cut into 1-inch-sized pieces. Place cookies on a greased cookie sheet and bake at 325°F for 10 minutes. Makes 12 cookies.

TUNA TIDBITS

One 6-ounce can of tuna
¼ cup water drained from tuna
3 tablespoons cooked egg white, chopped
¼ cup cornmeal
½ cup whole wheat flour

Preheat oven to 350°F. Combine tuna, egg white, and water. Add cornmeal and flour and blend to form a dough. Knead into a ball and roll to ¼-inch thick. Cut into 1-inch-sized pieces. Bake at 350°F for 20 minutes. Makes 12 cookies.

Dear Friends,

When Avon Books approached me with the idea of judging a contest to find a novella to publish along with *Family Affair*, I thought it was a fabulous idea. I know what it's like to be a struggling author. I tell writers' groups—and it's true—that I once got rejected so fast my manuscript hit me in the back of the head on my way home from the post office.

The process of picking the winner in this contest has a story of its own. The fine people at Avon Books narrowed down the submissions to three and sent them to me to pick the winner. The names were removed so I wouldn't know who'd submitted the manuscripts. When I received the final three to judge, my husband and I were on a trip with my brother. I settled down in the hotel room and read the stories. Each one was excellent in its own way, but "The Bet" had me smiling and cheering for the heroine. Of the three finalists, I found "The Bet" complemented my own story best, so I chose that one as the winner.

Now here's the kicker: I know the author, Darlene Panzera! She's a local writer in Washington State, who's been honing her craft for years.

Darlene reminds me a lot of myself when I was attempting to get published many years ago—eager and energetic, willing to sacrifice to pursue her dream. I am honored to have played a small part in her success. I know you'll enjoy her story. Remember her name, because you're going to be seeing it a lot in the coming years.

Okay, grab a cup of coffee or tea, take off your shoes, and curl up for two fun reads—Darlene's and mine. If you have a minute, log onto my Facebook page and share your thoughts on our stories.

Enjoy!
Debbie Macomber

One

JENNY CROSSED THE MAIN STREET OF THE rustic two-block town wishing she'd brought her shotgun. Or perhaps a bulldozer to knock the sleazy café and all its slimy bet-wagering occupants back into the infernal snake hole they came from. But even that wouldn't be good enough. Maybe the only thing to wipe the Bets & Burgers Café off the eastern slopes of the Washington Cascades would be a keg of dynamite.

She narrowed her gaze on the handful of men socializing in front of the café entrance.

"Marry me," David Wilson called out as she approached, "and I'll split the money with you fifty-fifty."

"I'll recite poetry every night," Kevin Forester promised.

"Marry me, Jenny," Charlie Pickett sang in

a rich tenor, "and I'll dedicate my first recorded song to you."

She clenched the fiberglass handle of the broomstick she carried with a grip that could break a mountain beaver's neck.

"Marry me, Jenny?" old Levi MacGowan asked, giving her a wink.

Jenny raised her brows. "Are you proposing to me, too, Levi?"

"You bet I am," he announced with a thump of his cane. "I figure I got as good a chance as the rest of them."

The cane slipped from Levi's hand and Jenny latched on to his arm so he wouldn't fall.

"See what a good wife you'd make?" Levi crowed.

"A good wife is more than a support post," Jenny countered, and retrieved the hand-carved wooden stick for him.

"Ouch!" Levi chuckled. "Feisty, today, are we?"

"Sorry, Levi. You know I love you," she said, and her tone softened, "but these other men—"

She shuddered. Only a high-stakes bet could bring this many people out at one o'clock on a hot Saturday afternoon. Heart hammering, she drew a deep breath and walked through the café door.

"Twenty dollars on Kevin," someone in the café shouted.

"Fifty says David can get Jenny to marry him," yelled another.

"Those two don't have a chance," said a man waving a fistful of money. "I'm betting on Charlie. He has a way with the ladies."

The run-down café hadn't changed since she'd last stepped foot in it six summers ago. Pete was still taking bets. His daughter, Irene, still sashayed her hips as she waited on the men and women sitting at the dozens of rough-hewn cedar tables. The same raucous laughter interrupted the music from the stereo. And the same bitter taste gathered at the back of her throat. Yep, nothing had changed, except she wasn't as young this time, wasn't as weak, wasn't as naïve . . .

"One hundred dollars on Ted Andrews," Pete bellowed as he faced the chalkboard. "Only a brave man can slap down that kind of cash." Then the café owner turned to search the crowd for more bets.

And spotted her.

"Pete, don't you dare duck behind that counter," she said, and pinned him with a sharp look.

The short bald-headed man responsible for the wagers straightened from his abrupt half-crouch. "Come to see who's in on the bet?"

"No." She marched toward the back of the room and raised the broomstick she'd borrowed from Sarah's Bakery. "I've come to teach you a lesson."

"Jenny!" Irene shrieked, grabbing hold of her arm. "Don't do it."

She shook the blond woman off, her mind reeling with horrific memories of the bets they'd placed six years earlier. Bets that left her standing alone at the altar. Bets that kept her from entering the café ever since.

Until *today*.

Using every ounce of her strength, Jenny swung the broomstick across the top of the counter.

Drink glasses shattered into a million glimmering pieces. An explosive, high-pitched crash pierced the room.

Then the chatter broke off, laughter died, and a bewildered hush ricocheted across the café. Every pair of eyes focused directly on her.

"Here you are, Pete," she said, and handed him the broom. "You'll need this to sweep up the mess."

Pete scowled. "You're going to have to pay for this."

She pointed to the chalkboard advertising her name in giant block letters. "The money from your bets should cover the damage."

Pete's face reddened. "That's not fair."

"Fair?" She scanned the scores of unapologetic faces, both male and female, that surrounded her. "You call making bets on my life *fair*?"

"Heck, Jenny, we all know your financial situation," Pete said with a shrug. "Now that the bank has given you a deadline, you'll have to marry to save Windy Meadows. And we're just placin' bets on who we think the lucky man is going to be."

"Marry?" Her mouth popped open.

"So far we have four main contenders: Charlie Pickett, Kevin Forester, David Wilson, and Ted Andrews."

"I don't need to marry anyone. I can just take in another investor."

"The last one took off with half a year's profit," yelled Charlie from the doorway.

Okay, so she'd lost out big on that one. She'd made a mistake. But there were other ways to save the ranch.

"I can sell off equipment at the upcoming auction."

"Your father sold everything he could before he died," Kevin said. "You don't have anything left."

"I have the cows," she said, lifting her chin, "and the horses. I came into town to hand out flyers advertising the guided pack trips I plan to lead up Wild Bear Ridge."

Pete's brow quirked. "You think pack trips will save Windy Meadows from foreclosure?"

"Four generations of my family are buried on that land," Jenny said, emphasizing each word. "Do you think I'm going to let anyone take *them* away from me?"

"You might not have a choice," David said, his voice quiet. "Unless you find the gold."

Gold? Jenny frowned. "What gold?"

"The gold your great-great grandfather discovered on the property," Pete explained.

"I don't know what you're talking about."

Pete pulled a printed page from behind the counter. "It's right here in this entry of his journal."

Jenny stared at the piece of paper. It was a photocopy of a page from her great-great grandfather's journal, all right. One of the old dusty volumes she'd loaned to the town historian the week before.

Pete pointed to the writing. "Ole Shamus O'Brien says here that the other guys found gold along the river bordering your property, but *he* found a gold mine. The entry is dated October twelfth, eighteen-eighty. A week later he passed away from pneumonia, and we're all guessing the gold is still there."

"If there was a gold mine hidden at Windy Meadows, I would know about it. I've covered every inch of that land and I . . ."

Right before the fire in the old barn took her father's life, he'd dug five holes on the far side of the property toward the western border. He'd said he wanted to plant trees. Trees he never bought. Did her father know what was in her great-great grandfather's journals? If he believed a gold mine was on the property, wouldn't he tell her?

149

"Is *that* why everyone wants to marry me?" Jenny demanded. "To get the gold?"

She knew better than to let her emotions take hold of her, but she couldn't help it. If there was one thing she couldn't stand, it was deception.

"You're despicable. All of you. Anyone with any decency at all, would loan me the money I need to save my land. But no. Here you are placing *bets*. And why? Because you believe there's a stupid gold mine on my property!" Her fists shook with mounting fury. "If you want something to believe, believe this—there isn't any man here who can get me to marry!"

A tall dark-haired man she had never seen before emerged through the crowd from across the room and slammed a green check down on the table beside her.

"Ten thousand dollars says you'll change your mind."

Jenny stared up at him. He topped her by at least six inches. Then she glanced down at the numbers scrawled on the check. A wave of openmouthed gasps rounded the room, followed by a single resounding, drawn-out whistle.

"What?" she demanded. Was this a joke?

"Ten thousand dollars says that within five weeks you'll marry *me*." Pushing back the brim of his black Stetson, he looked into her eyes with a look born of pure confidence.

"You—you must be out of your mind."

"I've never been more serious."

"So if I don't marry you, and I win," she said, flustered by the way his silver-gray eyes studied her, "I get your ten thousand."

"Yes."

"And if you win . . . ?"

"I get you."

She struggled to regain her composure. "What's your name?"

"Chandler," he said, never taking his eyes off her. "Nick Chandler."

"You're on." She accepted his challenge with outward calm, but her stomach twisted into a thousand knots, and her legs trembled with the need to run. Fast.

She turned to leave, but a hand on her shoulder spun her around and she found herself pressed up against her newly acquired opponent instead.

Her first thought was to reach down and

draw out her boot knife, but before she could react, his warm lips brushed across her own.

What perverse, mind-warping insanity led her to think she could stop the bets? Here, it was six years since the last time her name was on the chalkboard, and she hadn't learned her lesson. She was still humiliating herself in front of everyone in this confounded café!

"My money's on Chandler," old Levi Mac-Gowan's voice rang out as more gasps and guf-faws erupted around them.

She pushed away from the brash newcomer and retaliated with a slap. A hard slap. She caught her breath as the left side of his tanned face turned a glorious dark pink.

Chandler didn't flinch. The hit must have stung like the spines of a Devil's Club plant, yet it didn't stop him from smiling at her, or looking at her with that mischievous twinkle in his eye.

With all the courage she could muster, she held her head high and walked out the door.

❧   ❧   ❧

NICK STARED AFTER HER, TRANSFIXED BY HER FLEE-ing image. She wore no makeup. She didn't need to. With her flashing blue eyes and her auburn hair, she was a natural beauty. But it was the look of concern flickering across her face after she smacked his cheek that caught his attention.

A ranch hand he'd met at the café prior to Jenny's arrival slapped his back and placed a congratulatory beer in his hands. "Bolder than a bugling bull elk in rut," said Wayne Freeman, shaking his head. "A little too bold, if you ask me."

Nick grinned. "Care to bet on that?"

"Not if I want to keep my job." The sandy-haired man nodded toward the door. "You just butt horns with my boss."

❖   ❖   ❖

AFTER CHECKING INTO THE PINE HOTEL, THE ONLY one in the flea-sized town, Nick went to his room and called N.L.C. Industries. He glanced at the clock while listening to his cell phone ring, calculating the three-hour time difference between the east and west coast. It was after four thirty in New York, but his vice-president, Rob Murray, would still be there even on a Saturday.

"Did you meet with the O'Brien woman?" asked Rob, his tone anxious.

Nick rubbed the left side of his face. "Yeah, we just had our first encounter."

"And?"

"She may take a little more time than I anticipated. Instead of a weekend, I may have to stay out here in Washington a few weeks."

"Weeks? What if, after all that time, you still can't sweet-talk the land away from her?"

"I may have to do more than sweet-talk. When I got here I learned I'm not the only one interested in getting my hands on her property. Some of the locals are willing to marry her for it."

"Marriage?" Rob repeated. "You can't be serious."

"I don't see any other way. If I don't marry her, someone else will. Then we'll never get the land."

Nick recalled the honest emotion racing across the redheaded beauty's face. Jenny O'Brien was *not* like any of the other fake, flirting, foraging females he'd dealt with most of his life. As far as he could tell, there wasn't anything phony about her, something he found irresistibly refreshing. It also made him feel like a first-rate jerk for having to deceive her.

"Why you?" asked Rob. "Isn't there someone else who can seduce the woman?"

"No one I can trust to get the job done right."

"Of course," Rob said, his voice lit with amusement. "So who's going to run the company while you're gone?"

"You are. Think you can handle it?"

"Yes, sir!"

"I'll keep abreast of the finances from here on my laptop, but I might not be able to check in with you every day. And, Rob?"

"Yes?"

"Don't put your feet up on my desk. This is only temporary."

Rob laughed on the other end of the line. "Got it."

Next, Nick punched in the number to his younger sister, Billie. Now that he'd gained Miss O'Brien's attention, he needed a way to get close to her. Wayne Freeman had unknowingly given him a pretty good idea how to do it, and he was going to need Billie's help.

Two

ENNY LEANED FORWARD IN THE SADDLE AS Starfire prepared to jump. Her fingers firm and steady on the reins, she pressed her knees to the horse's side. Starfire's muscles bunched beneath her and they sailed into the air, clearing the gate by half a foot.

No doubt about it. The best remedy for stress was a good ride. Starfire landed and relief swept over her the same as when an airplane touched down on the runway. Not because she was afraid of flying but because she was home. On Windy Meadows property. Where everything was familiar. Everything was safe.

She brought the Thoroughbred's pace down to a slow trot, and headed straight for the stable. As she slid out of the saddle, the sweet smell of horse and hay soothed her senses. Neighs from the other horses blended together to sing her favorite song.

Why couldn't the townspeople understand her resolve to keep the ranch? Hadn't they ever loved anything so much it would kill them—rip out their heart and soul—to have to let it go?

And why did they think marriage was the only solution to her financial dilemma? Maybe they expected her to be like the other young women who either kicked off their cowgirl boots on the way to the city, or married the first guy who asked them to dance.

She wouldn't sell Windy Meadows. And she wouldn't hitch herself to a man she didn't love, no matter how good a dance partner.

The audacity of that conceited, dark-haired man to bet he could convince her to marry him! Nick Chandler didn't even know her.

And what kind of man kissed a complete stranger? He appeared to be in his early thirties and was dressed like the other ranchers wearing a T-shirt, jeans, and a black Stetson hat. But instead of dirt, sweat, and leather, he smelled like a new shirt straight from the package. And when he touched her . . . his hands were smooth. Too smooth to have done much ranch work. Could he be a city slicker out on vacation?

Whoever he was, he'd foolishly bet her ten thousand dollars, and the temptation to acquire some easy money had been too hard for her to resist. All she had to do was avoid the man for the last part of June and the first three weeks of July and the ten thousand would be hers. *Half her bank debt.*

Combined with the money she received from the pack trips, she'd be debt-free a full month before her end of summer deadline. Wouldn't *that* surprise everyone?

She'd love nothing better than to stay outside with the horses all day, but duty called, and a stack of bills waited for her in her father's office.

Jenny trudged up the back steps to the house and picked up the first envelope on the dark mahogany desk. Another buyout proposal from N.L.C. Industries. A quick toss into the trash can took care of that one. The next set of bills took more time.

Competition from other countries had caused the value of beef to drop and the change in climate patterns had also taken its toll. Yes, profits were down—way, way down—and she wasn't certain how to cut costs. She'd ridden horses most of her life and dabbled in medicine. She didn't have a degree in business. Why, if her father was still alive . . .

She swallowed hard. If her father *was* still alive, he would be the one struggling to balance the ranch's profit-and-loss statement.

Two hours later, Jenny shut off the computer and frowned at the sudden rise of voices below.

She leaned her head through the open second-story window and spotted a blue Ford pickup parked outside with a chrome finish so shiny it reflected the dirt in her driveway.

A thread of panic laced her steps as she hurried downstairs. Had N.L.C. sent another corporate front man to make her an offer in person? After waving a shotgun in the last guy's face, she hadn't expected them to return.

Ready to ambush the intrusive company representative with a verbal assault, she nearly ran straight into the young woman with short caramel-colored hair coming through the back door of her kitchen.

"Who are you?" Jenny asked.

"Billie."

She stared at the Yankee baseball cap and black Budweiser T-shirt the woman with the small boyish frame was wearing and the luggage in her hand.

"What are you doing here?"

"No idea." Billie scowled and pushed past her. "But right now I'm taking my suitcase to my room."

Did Uncle Harry invite this tomboy character here? And if he did, why didn't she know about it? Shaking her head, Jenny left the kitchen and went outside.

She took three steps across the porch—and locked gazes with the same silver-gray eyes she'd spent most of her sleep-tossed night trying to forget. She froze, her breath caught in her chest.

No. It couldn't be.

The dark-haired man with the black Stetson tipped the edge of his hat in greeting. Her Uncle Harry turned and motioned for her to join them.

"Jenny, I'd like you to meet—"

"Chandler." Saying his name was like chewing sour huckleberries.

"I've just hired him to be our new ranch manager," Harry said, sticking the shovel he was holding into the ground.

"What?" She began to feel claustrophobic, like the whole world was closing in on her. "But, Harry, *you* are the ranch manager."

"And you need me to accompany you on the pack trips. We need someone to look after the ranch for us, Jenny, and Nick's our man."

"Th-that man," she stammered, "bet ten thousand dollars he can get me to marry him."

Harry turned and leaned on the handle of the shovel. "Is that right?"

"Yes, sir," Nick Chandler informed him, clearly not intimidated by Harry's hard, scrutinizing look.

Jenny stared back and forth between them, breathless, and waited for her uncle to throw him off the ranch. Any minute now . . . *Any second . . .*

The corners of Harry's pale blue eyes crinkled, and he let out a hearty chuckle.

"Good luck, son," he said, extending his hand.

Chandler shook it. "Thank you, sir."

162

Jenny gasped, unable to believe her ears, and Chandler shot her a mischievous grin.

"So who is the girl in the house?" she asked, and her voice not only cracked but rose an octave.

"My sister Billie." Chandler's voice was deep and smooth.

"Billie's going to cook for us," Harry explained.

"Harry," she said, and stepped off the porch, "can we talk about this?"

Chandler's gaze followed her. His expression dared her to try to change Harry's mind. She returned his look with one of her own. One that said *Watch me* as she pulled her uncle away.

Harry Fisher, her mother's brother, came to live at Windy Meadows after his wife's funeral when Jenny was ten. Her father, who believed Harry possessed an impeccable ability to judge character, put him in charge of hiring the other ranch hands and never once questioned his choice of men. And neither had she. Until *now*.

She couldn't allow Harry to keep this man on the ranch, but she had to be careful not to step on his authority either. Harry took great pride in his decisions and she didn't want to hurt his feelings.

"I didn't know you planned to hire anyone," she said, keeping her voice soft so Chandler couldn't hear.

"I wasn't," Harry admitted. "Nick just showed up. He asked if we needed an extra hand and the more I talked to him, the more I thought about it."

"But ranch manager?" Jenny asked. "Do you really think he's qualified for that position?"

Harry put a big, burly arm around her shoulders.

"He's more than qualified. He and his sister grew up on their grandfather's ranch in upstate New York, and Nick used to ride rodeo."

This isn't working, Jenny thought, and bit her lower lip. She needed to change tactics.

"Harry, you know what a financial mess we're in. How can we afford to hire someone right now?"

"I'm going to give him my salary."

"But—"

He put up a hand to silence her protests. "What do I need money for? I have a bed to sleep in at night, food in my belly, breath in my lungs . . ."

"We could use your salary to save the ranch."

Harry shook his head. "Nick can help us save the ranch. He has a degree in business."

"A degree doesn't mean he's good."

"My gut instinct tells me he is."

"What about his sister?" she demanded.

"Nick says Billie is epileptic and he's responsible for her. He promises she can cook and help out in the stable for free, if we let her stay here with him."

"She's another mouth to feed."

"Ah, but not a big one."

Jenny peeked over Harry's shoulder as Nick Chandler and his tiny sister took more luggage out of the truck. Their contrast in size was so great, she wouldn't have believed they were related except for the identical silver-gray eyes.

Harry followed her gaze. "I gave them the two extra bedrooms upstairs."

"You invited them to sleep in the house?"

"Well, I couldn't have Billie sleep in the bunkhouse with all the men. It wouldn't be right."

"Okay," Jenny said, and threw up her hands. "Why can't *Chandler* sleep in the bunkhouse?"

"He says he needs to stay close to his sister at night." Harry shrugged. "Says she has nightmares."

"Nightmares," Jenny repeated, and pursed her lips. She didn't believe a word of it.

Billie appeared to be about her own age. Twenty-eight? But the young woman's attire, scowl, and belligerent tone during their encounter on the stairs reminded her of a juvenile delinquent. Tough. With attitude.

"I can't imagine that girl being afraid of *anything*," Jenny said, shaking her head.

"Why does it matter where they sleep?"

"I don't want that man anywhere near me, that's why."

"Afraid he might win the bet?" Harry's blue eyes twinkled.

"Of course not."

"Then there's no problem."

"Yes, there is," Jenny said. "I'm sorry, Harry, but I insist he goes."

"And *I insist he stays*."

"But—" Jenny stared at her uncle as he

THE BET

planted his boots, drew himself up, and appeared ten feet taller. She swallowed hard, sure she felt her nerves tremble.

"Jenny," Harry said, using a tone she hadn't heard since she was a child. "I need him."

Need him? She hesitated. Her uncle didn't need anybody, but he was keeping something from her. And she was too afraid to ask why.

"Give him a week," Harry said, his voice firm, "then you can fire him if you want to."

"One week," she agreed.

Her uncle smiled, and turned back into the man she'd always known and loved. "Thank you, Jenny. It will all work out, you'll see."

Uncle Harry headed toward the corrals and Jenny wiped her sweaty hands down the sides of her jeans.

One week. Then she'd get some answers.

❁   ❁   ❁

BILLIE STRUGGLED TO HAUL HER OTHER SUITCASE UP the narrow flight of wooden stairs in the big cedar house.

"I thought a ranch was supposed to only have one floor," she complained.

Nick didn't let her sour mood bother him.

In fact, his plan had worked so well, he was springing up the steps.

"This is a farmhouse," he said, and took the suitcase from his sister's hands. "Did you see how big the kitchen is?"

"Of course, since that's where I'm supposed to prepare everyone's meals. How could you do this to me? You know I can't cook."

"Then it's time you learned."

"I won't do it," she said, jutting out her jaw.

Sometimes Billie could irritate him to no end.

"How else could I convince them to let you come to the ranch with me?"

"I don't know. I thought that crazy story about me being epileptic was pretty good," she said, her hands on her hips. "Nick, we don't belong here. This is never going to work, and now you've wasted ten thousand dollars on a stupid bet—"

"The bet drew Jenny O'Brien's attention."

"It sure did," Billie drawled. "I think she hates you."

"Billie," he pleaded, and glanced down the stairs to make sure no one was listening, "the only reason I'm doing this is for *you*. You're the one with the hundred-thousand-dollar gambling debt. Do you have any idea what Victor Lucarelli will do to you if you don't get the money to pay him back?"

"I'd rather not think about it." Billie's face blanched. "I made a mistake."

"Two mistakes," he corrected. "First you cheated the casino owner—didn't even *think* the security camera might catch you in the act, and then you lost all his money to someone else."

"It was supposed to be a private game of poker and I was mad at Lucarelli for being so haughty." His sister's eyes widened. "Nick . . . do you think Lucarelli and his men will kill me?"

"They'd have to kill *me* first," he said fiercely.

"I'm sorry." Billie sounded more sincere than he'd ever heard her. "I'm so sorry."

"I know." He drew in a deep breath and led her into the privacy of his bedroom. "If I can win the bet and get Jenny to marry me, the O'Brien land will be half mine. I'll have the missing piece of acreage I need to sell my land tracts to Davenport. Not only will we have the money to pay off your debt, but we'll have money to buy Jenny another ranch to live on."

Billie shrugged. "So what do you want me to do?"

"Become Jenny's friend," he said, nudging his sister with his shoulder. "From what I've learned from the people in town, she could use a good friend. Find her weak spots. Give me an edge so I can get close to her."

"You never needed my help with a woman before," Billie teased. "Do you really think you can get her to marry you?"

Nick grinned. "Go study some cookbooks."

Three

AFTER A RESTLESS NIGHT'S SLEEP, JENNY AWOKE early, threw on a pair of jeans and an old T-shirt, and tied her long hair up in a ponytail.

Had she overreacted to her uncle's decision to hire Chandler? The work on the ranch kept everyone busy from sunup to sundown. Surely the chances of the man having any spare time to bother her would be slim.

She was wrong. Nick Chandler fell into step beside her as she made her way down to the stable.

"How about you and I go for a ride this evening? You could show me the layout of the land on horseback."

"That's Harry's job," she said, and then cast him an appraising look. "Besides, you won't be up to it."

"What's that supposed to mean?"

"It means those smooth hands of yours, which are no doubt accustomed to delicate office work, will be covered in blisters by nightfall. You won't be able to hold on to the reins long enough for an evening ride."

Chandler looked as if she'd punched him in the gut.

"If I *am* able to hold on to the reins," he said, shooting her a sideways glance, "will you ride with me?"

"No."

"Why not?"

"I don't want to."

Jenny's twelve-year-old neighbor, Josh Hanson, ran between them. "The only one who can get a date with Jenny is *me.* She gives me riding lessons every Monday."

Nick tipped his hat toward the boy. "Great idea."

"Forget it, Chandler," Jenny warned and turned toward Josh. "Saddle Echo and meet me in the arena."

Josh ran off, and when Jenny reached the stable she found Harry arguing with Frank Delaney.

"Managing a ranch is hard work," Harry

shouted. "I need someone who will take on a challenge, not hide behind it. I need someone assertive."

"Well, you certainly are assertive," Jenny muttered, and glanced at the dark-haired man beside her.

"I heard that," said Chandler, giving her a wink.

"I'll show you assertive," said Frank. His upper lip curled as Chandler approached. "We'll just see who the better man is."

Frank snatched a saddle off the rack and went out the back door in a huff.

"He's going to be a problem," Jenny predicted.

"Nah. He'll cool down in a couple of days." Harry took a brown leather bridle from one of the hooks along the wall. "What do you think? Should we have Nick ride Satan?"

She hesitated. Satan had been her father's horse. Although he desperately needed to be exercised, the temperamental black quarter horse had been difficult to control since her father's death six months ago. She doubted Nick Chandler could stay on him ten minutes, let alone a full day in the fields.

"No, I don't think he could handle him."

"I can handle any horse you give me," Chandler insisted.

How could he be so sure he could handle an animal he knew nothing about? In her opinion, it was high time Nick Chandler got knocked down a notch. Riding Satan would probably knock his bolstered ego down *several* notches. Would it be enough to make him quit?

"Yes," Jenny said, amusement bubbling up within her, "let's put him on Satan."

❧   ❧   ❧

AFTER JENNY GAVE YOUNG JOSH A RIDING LESSON, she handed the reins of a small pinto over to Billie. "Be gentle," she warned. "My horses respond to voice commands and don't need extra kicks or excessive tugs on the reins."

"I promise I won't hurt him," Billie said, hoisting herself into the saddle.

"Are you sure you can ride?"

For a moment, Billie looked like she was about to lash into her with an assortment of colorful language, but then the young woman took a deep breath and replied, "Yes, I can ride."

Billie told the truth. The young woman

kept up with an easy gait, and maneuvered the pinto quite well when they circled a small group of cows at the far end of the field.

Even more of a surprise was the way Billie's brother systematically drove the scattered herd into one large group. Jenny paused for a moment to watch.

Where did he learn to maneuver hairpin turns like that? On the rodeo circuit? Racing back and forth, as if one with his steed, Nick Chandler dominated the field. Jenny straightened in her saddle. Rarely had she seen such expert precision—even in skilled professionals.

"Got to admit, he's good," Wayne said, riding up beside her.

"Harry only hires the best."

Billie rode toward them with a stray calf and Wayne called out, "You're too small for ranch work."

Billie scrunched her nose and lifted her chin. "And you're too *sweet*."

Jenny laughed. "Wayne Freeman, meet Billie Chandler."

❖   ❖   ❖

Nick eased forward in the saddle to adjust his tired seat. His thighs ached, his back ached, his hands were raw, and to top it off, he *did* have a few blisters. Jenny would feel smug about that.

What was he doing on this pitiful run-down ranch? He was a businessman with contracts to sign. He didn't belong here and the other ranch hands made darn sure he knew it.

Every available moment, they'd drive the cattle in different directions. At lunch they filled his saddlebag with manure, and in the afternoon one of them drove a tractor through the fence he'd fixed.

"It's one thing to try to woo some girl," said Wayne Freeman, all the friendliness from the café absent from his face, "and another to think you can worm yourself onto this ranch and tell us what to do. Frank and I were here long before you strolled into town. Even little Josh has more experience than you."

Even worse than the ranch hands' disloyalty was the fact Jenny planned to lead some of the other bet-wagering cowboys on an overnight pack trip into the mountains.

Harry said Jenny expected families and 4-H groups to sign up for her pack trips. When the men from the café signed up instead, she'd almost backed out. Except each pack trip could bring in two thousand dollars and she needed the money. Nick shook his head, despair seeping into every muscle of his overexerted body.

Harry was going with her. Still, the other men would have a better shot at winning the bet—unless he gained her affection first. That incredible feat was going to require every ounce of charm he could muster, and at the moment, he wasn't sure he was up to it.

As he drove the last of the cattle into the corral for the night, Nick forced Satan to a halt and the black gelding snorted with annoyance. If it wasn't the ranch hands testing him, it was the horse. At least the horse finally knew who was boss.

Pushing his hat off his forehead, Nick wiped the sweat from his brow with the back of his hand . . . and saw Jenny sitting on the top rail of the corral fence.

She waved to him, an eager expression upon her face, almost as if she'd been anticipating his arrival. He must be mistaken. He turned and looked behind him but no one else was around.

He slid out of the saddle as she approached and fed Satan another of the special horse treats he'd used as bribery to keep him under control. When his feet hit the solid ground, he feared his limp legs would buckle, but he wasn't going to let *her* know that.

"Come to check on me?" he asked, managing a grin as he closed the corral gate and secured the lock.

"Heck no. I came to check on the horse." Jenny took the reins from his hands and ran her fingers down one of the animal's front legs. But contrary to her claim, her eyes were on him and not Satan.

"Care to go on that ride with me?" he asked, knowing full-well she'd refuse.

"Yes, I would."

"You *would*?" He swallowed hard. Climbing back up into the saddle would be like climbing N.L.C. Industries New York office tower—without any superhero strength.

Jenny fed Satan a carrot and then turned to look at him, her bright blue eyes sparkling with mischief. What was she up to? Then a brilliant smile escaped her lips and he found it didn't matter. It was the first real smile he'd seen on her.

His heart rate doubled, and his resolve hardened. This was the chance he'd been waiting for, the chance to spend time alone with her, and for that he would hoist himself back into that saddle or die trying.

A few minutes later, Jenny led two fresh horses from the stable and handed him the reins of a feisty chestnut that had its teeth fully exposed and its ears pinned back.

"Don't you have any horses with a calm disposition?" he asked, unable to keep the irritation out of his voice.

"Of course," she said, another smile parting her lips. "I just thought an expert wrangler, such as yourself, would prefer to ride a horse with a little more spirit."

"Spirit? Is that what you call this?" he said, pointing to the animal's threatening stance.

Jenny laughed, and he suddenly had a pretty good idea why she agreed to ride with him. *Torture.*

❖   ❖   ❖

ROUNDING THE UPPER LOOP TRAIL, JENNY FROWNED as Nick Chandler coaxed the wild chestnut into an easy lope. How did he *do* it? She had never been able to control that horse, but she wasn't going to let *him* know that.

Jenny sensed Chandler gaining speed behind her.

"Race you!" she called, and pushed Starfire forward with a slight squeeze of her legs.

She rode parallel to the river and couldn't help scan the embankment. If her great-great grandfather had found a goldmine, where could it be?

Ahead, the logjam jump came into view. Leaning forward, she adjusted her weight in the saddle. Starfire soared into the air like a pro and landed on the other side with a soft thud.

Seconds later, a startled whinny pierced the air, and when Jenny looked back, Chandler was lying on the ground. Slowing Starfire, she slid out of the saddle and ran across the meadow to his side. He wasn't moving.

Panic coursed through her limbs, making her tremble. She shouldn't have tried to race him, shouldn't have brought him out here. She knew he had been in no condition to ride after his work in the saddle all day. What if he suffered a concussion? Or broke his neck?

He lay face up with his eyes closed, and

didn't appear to be breathing. She had trouble breathing herself as she pressed her fingers to his throat and checked for a pulse.

Thank God, he was still alive. She recalled the new medical guidelines she'd seen on the Internet and gave him thirty hard, fast chest presses to keep his blood circulating. Then she tilted his chin up and opened his mouth with her finger. Nothing seemed to be blocking the airway. She pinched his nose closed. Took a deep breath. Lowered her mouth to his to perform CPR.

She was about to blow air into his lungs when the world rolled over, placing Chandler on top, with a very dark, calculating look in his eyes.

Jenny thrust Chandler off to the side, pulled out her boot knife, and sprang to her feet. "You faked that fall on *purpose*."

"And *you*," he said, pointing to the crazed horse prancing about the field, "deliberately put me on that beast to torture me. What are you going to do now? Stab me?"

She followed his gaze to the tip of her boot knife, its sharp point glistening orange from the setting sun. What was she thinking?

"I—I'm sorry," she said, and trembled as she sheathed the knife beneath the hem of her jeans. "You seem to bring out the worst in me."

"Oh, well, you know what they say," Chandler said, pulling himself off the ground.

"What?" she demanded. Had the townspeople been talking about her again? "What do they say?"

"There's a fine line between love and hate."

"In your case," she said, hardening her expression, "that fine line is a brick wall."

She walked away from him and headed toward the giant apple tree fifty feet away.

"Where are you going?" Nick asked, following her.

"The cemetery."

There was no gate. Jenny swept her gaze over the names carved into the headstones, and knelt beside the newest, the one without any moss or age spots. The grave of her father, George O'Brien.

"There's so many of them."

Chandler's voice was filled with awe. What did he expect from a family cemetery?

Jenny tossed a few rotten apples that had fallen from the tree above away from the graves. Then she pointed to the oldest stone, which was also the smallest. "My great-great grandfather Shamus O'Brien left Ireland in eighteen seventy-six with his wife and young son. He traveled across America to Washington State, built the ranch, and then died in eighteen-eighty during the area's second short gold boom."

"The man with the gold," Nick commented.

Jenny pointed to another grave farther to the right. "This is my grandfather, Sean O'Brien. When I was little, he sat me on his knee and told me the reason they buried family on the property was to ensure the land would never be sold. Never slip into the hands of developers. He said he'd rest easy knowing the land would always belong to one of his descendants."

"That's why you won't sell," Nick said, and ran a hand through his hair.

"No, I won't sell," Jenny said, and turned to face him straight on. "So if you think you can come here, and marry me, and sell the land out from under me, you can forget it."

"What if I just want to ranch?" Nick asked. "What if I'm just so taken with your beauty that I'd like to stay here forever . . . with you."

Jenny smirked and rolled her eyes. "I know you must have an ulterior motive for betting me the ten thousand. I also know how valuable the land could be, if I didn't owe so much debt. I've had offers from several large companies to buy the land."

"Which ones?" Nick asked, crossing his arms over his chest.

"N.L.C. Industries is the most bothersome." Jenny scowled. "I'm beginning to think there isn't anything that company won't do to get their hands on my land."

Nick chuckled. "I've heard they are tenacious."

"Tenacious isn't even the word." She blew out a huff of disgust. "The company is in league with the devil."

"That bad?" Nick raised his brows.

"Oh, yes," she assured him. "Rumor has it the company needs to sell the properties it purchased here in Pine. Except *my* land sits smack in the middle of theirs, and no prospective buyer wants a useless donut-hole tract. They want my land, Windy Meadows, included in the deal."

"Sounds like N.L.C. Industries is screwed," Nick said, nodding his head.

"Serves them right for purchasing land around me in the first place, thinking they could run me out and build some smog-ridden industrial plant," Jenny retorted. Her blood boiled and her heart pounded just talking about it. "Do you know last month N.L.C. had the gall to offer to have the graves of my family relocated?"

"That's awful," Nick agreed.

"Where would they move them?" Jenny demanded, rising to her feet. "My family doesn't belong in some public cemetery on the other side of town. This is their home, the place they lived and loved and watched their children grow. Can you imagine seeing the caskets of your loved ones being pulled from the ground, unearthed from—" Unable to continue, Jenny shuddered.

"I imagine it would be haunting," Nick said, his face drawn, as if he too was affected by the image.

"Ghastly," Jenny amended. "No, I don't have any sympathy for N.L.C. Industries. As far as I'm concerned, they've dug their own grave."

❊　❊　❊

THE LATE EVENING HEAT BORE DOWN ON THE RANCH with wicked intentions, leaving everyone in desperate need of a cold shower and a really good meal.

Jenny approached the picnic tables, and when Chandler turned toward her, she hesitated in midstep. Chandler's direct gaze electrified every nerve in her body. How could she ignore him when he looked at her like that?

Self-conscious, she turned her attention to her lanky red-bearded cousin who sat beside Wayne Freeman.

"Patrick, what brings you here?"

Her cousin smirked. "I heard you got someone to replace Wayne's feeble attempts in the kitchen and thought I'd come for a good dinner."

"You don't like the way I cook?" Wayne asked, a wide unaffected smile spreading across his face.

"Hate to break it to ya," Patrick told him, "but there's a reason your restaurant failed."

"Yes, there is," Wayne agreed, "but it wasn't because of the taste of the food."

"You're a chef?" Nick asked.

"Was. Past-tense." Wayne shifted his jaw

and looked him square in the eye. "But I'm sure your sister is a much better cook than I am."

Jenny watched Nick glance toward Billie, his expression tense. Did he doubt his sister's ability?

Patrick poked her arm. "Where's Harry?"

"He went to bed early. We had to round up the cows from the entire hillside and we're all exhausted."

"Me too." Patrick's smile faded. "The real reason I came tonight is to say goodbye. I sold my ranch to Stewart Davenport."

"*No!*" Jenny shook her head, her stomach contracted into a tight ball. "Patrick, how could you?"

"I don't have the money to keep my ranch, not in this economy."

"You don't have to go," Jenny protested. "You can stay here with us and be our new ranch manager."

She glanced at Chandler and he gave her a dark look. But wouldn't Harry prefer family over a stranger for the position? Patrick could be the answer to her problems.

"I'm sorry, Jenny, but I'm done ranching. Besides, you've taken in enough homeless cowboys." His gaze swept over Nick, Wayne, Frank, and little Josh, who sat quietly at the end of the table. "No offense, guys."

"None taken. If it weren't for Windy Meadows . . ." Wayne shook his head. "Where will you go?"

"I thought I'd head down to California for a while, lie on the beach, maybe give surfing a try."

"But this is your *home*," Jenny exclaimed.

Patrick slouched forward. "Lately, I don't even know what it is I'm working for."

"For *this*." Jenny swept her hand toward the rich sun-gold meadows, pine-scented evergreens, and granite peaks stretching into a vibrant finger-painted sky. "We work for this."

"It's not enough. I want something more."

What more was there? She didn't understand.

"From now on, home will be wherever I hang my hat." A sudden gleam entered Patrick's eyes. "I want to enjoy life, not work so hard I don't know what day it is."

"Here, here!" said Wayne, lifting his mug in a toast.

"I want to wake each morning with something to look forward to," Patrick continued, "and go to bed each night with someone to keep me warm."

"Here, here!" the others at the table chorused.

Jenny's throat tightened. How could he just pick up and leave? If Patrick wanted someone to warm his bed at night, why didn't he just get a dog?

Drat! A tear spilled over the rim of her left eye. She hoped no one would notice, but when she wiped her cheek with her hand, she saw someone *did* notice. Double drat! Nick Chandler noticed everything.

She turned her head, spotted the large smoking tray in Billie's hands, and stifled a groan. Could the night get any worse? Jenny glanced around at the others, her stomach clenched, and she braced for the next wave of disaster.

Patrick's jaw dropped. "What are we having?"

"Charcoal, by the looks of it," said Frank with a sneer.

"It's a . . . a roast." Billie set the tray down on the table. "It's just a little . . . well done."

"Overdone," Wayne amended. "Where did you go to culinary school?"

"I didn't," Billie said, and bit her lip.

"Then how," asked Wayne, "did you learn to cook such a mouth-watering piece of . . . uh . . . whatever it is?"

The men laughed and Jenny looked past Billie's hard-nosed expression to the wounded look in her eyes.

Jenny knew that look. It was the same look she'd seen in the mirror after she'd been laughed at, *ridiculed*, by the men who placed bets at the Bets & Burgers Café six years before.

First there had been one laugh. Then another. Followed by two more until the laughter joined together like a thunderous stampede. Round and round it went, racing from one end of the room to the other, devouring every shred of self-confidence she'd ever possessed.

"*Stop!* It's not Billie's fault." She choked on her words and caught a surprised look from Wayne. "I think the temperature gauge on the oven is broken."

Billie stared at her. Jenny stared back, but instead of the young woman's difference in size and appearance, all she saw was herself.

Maybe it was because Patrick's announcement had left her vulnerable. Or perhaps it was her mind playing tricks on her. All she knew, at that moment, was that she and Billie were the *same*.

❖   ❖   ❖

NICK ROSE AT FOUR A.M. AND DISCOVERED AN URGENT e-mail message from the previous day on his computer. Ten seconds later he had his vice president at N.L.C. Industries on the phone.

"Vic Lucarelli called," said Rob. "He's not happy you and Billie took off. He thinks you're hiding her—trying to get her out of the country or something. He says if you don't get him his money within the next three weeks, he's going to have to take serious measures."

Nick's jaw clenched as he pictured the ruthless casino owner in his head. Slick black hair, tanned features, beady dark eyes—the man was exactly the type one would expect to meet in a back alley. Why his sister thought she could cheat the guy at a private game of cards, he didn't know. All he *did* know was that he had to protect her."

"Rob, did you tell Lucarelli I can get him the

money Billie owes him as soon as I sell these Northwest land parcels to Mr. Davenport?"

"Yeah."

"And?" Nick held his breath and could almost hear Rob squirm during the brief hesitation that stretched between them.

"He expects results."

❧   ❧   ❧

JENNY PULLED THE COVERS HIGHER, HOPING TO catch a few more minutes of sleep before chores needed to be done. A few more minutes of . . .

Her heart rate doubled as she sprang straight up in bed. She'd dreamed about him last night. As much as she hated to admit it, Nick Chandler had entered her dreams . . . and *kissed* her. She could almost feel . . . She ran a finger over her lower lip and shook her head.

So what if he was the best rider she had ever seen? She'd fallen for rodeo stars before and it brought nothing but trouble. No, she couldn't allow herself to lose focus. She needed to win the bet. Harry had asked her to give Chandler a week, but she couldn't allow the handsome cowboy to stay another day.

Jenny dressed and, once outside, squinted

against the bright sun as she scanned the fields.

She spotted Harry's white hair at the far end of the pasture and marched toward him, fists clenched. Harry would listen to her this time and there was nothing that dream-invading Casanova cowboy could do about it. Chandler would be off the ranch within the hour.

Jenny quickened her pace and kept her eyes on her uncle. Harry began to swing the hammer, then he clutched at his arm and staggered backward as if stung. She'd warned him about the bees by that fence.

But a man doesn't keel over from a bee sting.

"Harry?" Jenny broke into a run. *"Harry!"*

Four

NICK RAN PAST JENNY AND DROPPED TO THE ground next to the old man's body. Harry wasn't moving. Ripping open his employer's shirt, he bent his head to listen for a heartbeat.

Jenny fell down on her knees beside them. "Dear God, no."

"He's alive." Nick straightened and glanced at her ashen face. "Jenny, I need your help."

At first she didn't respond. She appeared dazed, as if in shock, and he shook her hard.

Then she motioned him aside, and proceeded to check his vitals. "His pulse is faint. His airway is clear, but he's not breathing."

"I need thirty chest compressions, like this." Jenny placed her hands together and pumped her uncle's chest. "I'll give two breaths, and then you continue the compressions."

195

Nick nodded and followed her lead. He'd never given anyone CPR. When her uncle failed to respond, he wondered if it was his fault. "Should I press harder?"

"No." She lifted her head. "You're doing fine. I think he's . . . Oh, dear God, he's turning blue."

Nick glanced at Harry's marbled face, and despite the intense heat beating down upon them, an icy drop of sweat ran down the length of his spine.

"We've got to get him to the hospital." His hands pumped Harry's chest a bit faster. "The farm truck?"

"Still broken. Wayne drove his pickup into town for supplies. Yours?"

"Billie took it to buy groceries."

Jenny's face fell. "The neighbors are gone for the weekend and Harry will never make it if we have to wait for an ambulance. The hospital is forty-five minutes away."

"I can cut the time in half."

"How?"

Harry's entire body shook, startling them both, and Nick realized he was trying to cough.

"Hang on, Harry." Tears streamed down

Jenny's cheeks as her uncle's eyes fluttered open. "Please, hang on."

"Sorry." The whisper hung softly on Harry's lips as his right hand inched across the ground to grasp hers.

Nick swallowed hard. He couldn't let the old man die. But what would he tell Jenny when she saw N.L.C.'s logo on the helicopter? He hit the first number on his cell phone.

"Sam," he said, his voice hoarse, "I need a chopper at the O'Brien ranch. *Now!*"

❁   ❁   ❁

JENNY SWAYED OVER HARRY'S STILL FORM AS THE helicopter angled to the right. If it weren't for the sharp metal buckle of the seat belt biting into her middle, she'd never believe any of it was real. How could her big strong uncle be so weak? How could they be flying, instead of driving, to the hospital in Wenatchee?

Just minutes before, the helicopter had swooped over the southern hillside. Its blades whirred like a monstrous hummingbird. As it set down in the field, the propeller's wind whipped at her hair and her clothes. She'd tried to step back. Instead, she tripped and fell on her butt into the dirt. When she looked up, the horrible blue-and-green spiral stared her in the face. The hateful emblem of N.L.C. Industries, the company trying to take the ranch. Her first impulse had been to jump back even farther. Then Nick reminded her Harry's life was on the line.

She looked over at the hard-faced G.I. Joe look-alike at the controls of the chopper. According to Nick, it was a lucky coincidence his pilot friend, Sam Reynolds, was in town. Sam didn't work for N.L.C. Industries, but the company had brought him in to evaluate the airstrip they'd acquired. Nick sat beside him, pushing buttons and monitoring data, as if they'd worked together their whole lives.

"Radio the hospital in Wenatchee," Nick instructed Sam. "Tell them to call Dr. Carlson."

Frowning, Jenny leaned forward and placed her hand on Nick's arm to gain his attention. "Who is Dr. Carlson?"

"Harry's cardiologist."

Jenny stared at him, openmouthed, unable to speak.

Nick gave her a swift compassionate look. "He didn't want you to worry."

"He told you? You *knew* about this?"

"It's the reason he hired me."

Her thoughts flew back to Nick's first day on the ranch. No wonder Harry had insisted they keep him. Her throat ran dry as guilt squeezed the air from her lungs. All this time she'd been trying to make Nick quit, she'd only been thinking of herself.

"Oh God," she said, her eyelids stinging. "I'm so sorry."

❀　❀　❀

TWENTY MINUTES LATER, THE EMERGENCY CREW carried Harry out of the back of the chopper on a stretcher and wheeled him into the emergency room. The admitting nurse told Jenny to remain in the waiting area and Nick led her over to a couch to sit down.

The familiar sterile stench trapped between the boxed walls made her nauseous. She'd been in the hospital too many times for too many dying loved ones. Today the odious scent hit her harder than ever before. Harry was all she had left. What would she do without him?

A woman handed her a pen and a clipboard full of forms, but her vision blurred until she could hardly see the paper. *Don't cry*, she told herself. *Force it back.*

The minute hand on the clock took a full turn before the double doors separating her from Harry opened and Dr. Carlson called her name.

She jumped to her feet. "How is he?"

"Harry suffered a mild heart attack. One of the three coronary arteries is blocked eighty-five percent and he'll need surgery to open it back up." Dr. Carlson's eyes filled with concern when he looked at her. "Did he mention any heart-related symptoms he might have had during the last few days?"

"No. He said nothing."

Beside her, Nick shifted his feet. "He's had occasional twinges of pain in his chest. Last night he said his left arm bothered him and he didn't feel well. He told me he meant to make an appointment to see you next week."

"He should have called sooner." Dr. Carlson shook his head. "Harry's last appointment with me was three months ago. I gave him some pills to thin his blood and told him to stop working so hard. I don't suppose the stubborn old coot listened to me."

Jenny's throat constricted into a painful knot as she thought about the way Harry rose at five A.M. every morning to work the fields, mend the fences, and herd the cattle. If she'd known about his heart condition, she never would have let him work another day in his life. She would have taken away his cigars, made him rest, insisted he eat properly.

No wonder he hadn't told her. If there was one thing Harry couldn't stand, it was being babied.

"The surgery will take hours," said Nick as they sat back down. "Would you like to go for coffee, or—?"

"I want to stay."

Her mind replayed Harry's collapse in the field and for one terrified moment, Jenny wondered what she would have done if Nick hadn't been there to help. There was no way she could have lifted Harry herself, and with the ranch hands gone, and no vehicle . . .

"Nick, I want to thank you for . . . what you've done. You saved his life."

"You're the one who saved him. Where did you learn CPR?"

"Medical school," she whispered.

201

He gave her a startled look. Perhaps he hadn't expected a poor country girl like her to have had much schooling.

"I didn't graduate. I came home after my third year when the money got tight. I had always planned to go back and finish, but then six months ago, my father died and I took over the ranch."

"Where's the rest of your family?"

"My grandparents and my mom . . . they're all . . . buried beneath the apple tree in the northeast corner of the property."

A fearsome ache wrenched the pit of her stomach. An ache similar to the one she'd experienced when she was very small and lost in the woods for the first time.

She had no one she could turn to. No one except Starfire, and she needed more than the companionship of a horse right now.

The pressure inside her head strained against her skull, her lungs tightened against her rib cage.

She was alone. Absolutely, unbearably . . . alone.

Nick wrapped his arm around her, and she

jumped at his touch. He studied her with an expression she couldn't quite place. Compassion? Sympathy? What it was, she didn't know, but when she looked into his eyes she was drawn into the silver-gray depths—and for one timeless second . . . it was almost as if he understood her.

"Shhh," he whispered against her ear. "Let it go."

She didn't have the strength to protest. She needed to be held, even if it *was* by the man who had bet against her. She collapsed against his chest. The fear and loneliness trapped inside her burst like a broken dam, and wracked her body with deep agonizing sobs.

❧   ❧   ❧

NICK STROKED THE BACK OF HER LONG AUBURN HAIR, and as the hour drew on, Jenny quieted. His own raw emotions flooded over him as he thought of the similarities between Harry and his father.

Both were men of integrity, rooted in their own beliefs—and working as if there were no tomorrow.

"My father told me someday we'd be partners and run the largest company in the nation."

Jenny raised her head and he realized he'd spoken the words aloud.

"He spent endless days . . . and nights . . . designing blueprints for buildings, researching products, running the numbers." Nick paused, smiling to himself. "He said he was doing it all for me and our future business."

"He must have really loved you."

"Billie thinks so. She was jealous he didn't include her in the plans."

"Is that why she tries to be a tomboy?"

"Nah. I think it has more to do with the fact she was the only girl on my grandfather's ranch after we lost our parents . . . on New Year's Eve."

"What happened?" Jenny's tears subsided and she wiped her eyes on his shirt.

Not that he minded. Her tears cooled his skin, and soothed the bitter taste of the memory. "A drunk driver hit their car head on."

"I'm sorry." She began to push away from him, as if realizing for the first time she was on top of him.

He continued to hold her tight. "Sometimes I wonder what my life would be like if they were still alive. The business I built is very different than the one my father planned. Over-extended loans and indecisive shareholders can lock up a company's cash flow for months. It's hard to get money when you need it."

She leaned back against his chest. "Is that why you want my land? You hope to find the gold everyone thinks is buried on my property to get a little extra cash?"

Nick grinned. "All I want is to marry you. Is that so hard to accept?"

Jenny nodded, her face solemn. "Yes."

"Why?"

"Six years ago I was engaged to Travis Koenig. The night before the wedding . . . Travis celebrated his bachelor party at the Bets & Burgers Café. He had been drinking, dancing with Irene Johnson, and the other men taunted him. They said he'd lost his edge with women since he started dating me. They bet Travis couldn't get Irene to sleep with him as a 'last fling.' Ian took the bet."

Nick scowled, and urged her to continue.

"I arrived at the church expecting a fairytale wedding . . . and Travis never came. I had to stand there . . . and face over a hundred pitying guests . . . alone."

"How did you find out about the bet?" Nick asked.

"I crossed the street to the café, saw the names on the chalkboard, found Travis upstairs—not alone. When I came back down, the men at the Bets & Burgers Café laughed. They didn't care about me. They just laughed and laughed."

"That's why you hate the café," Nick said, and caressed her wrist in a soothing circular motion.

"I thought if I could hide away on the ranch, my life would be okay." Jenny swallowed the lump in her throat and continued, "Then six months ago my father died when the old barn caught fire." She paused and shook her head. "I've been struggling to make ends meet, but I'm in debt way over my head . . . and I found out late last night the bank manager has moved up my foreclosure date. If I can't bring my account current by July sixteenth, he's going to take my ranch."

"No, he won't," Nick said, his voice firm

and strong. "I won't let him. We'll go over the ranch's files, books, records—whatever you've got—and we'll figure something out . . . trust me, Jenny."

"You bet against me. Why would I ever trust you?"

"You and I are more alike than you can imagine."

❧   ❧   ❧

It was nearly nightfall when Harry came fully awake.

"Hey, Harry." Jenny leaned forward in the straight-backed chair beside his bed and touched his cheek. The lines of his face had deepened and his eyes were circled by dark shadows, but at least his skin no longer resembled blueberry cheesecake. "Dr. Carlson says the surgery went well, but the nurses are all hoping to keep you here a few more days. Did you flirt with them in the operating room?"

"I'm too old to flirt." Her uncle cracked a small grin. Then his face took on a worried expression. "I didn't mean to scare you."

"Me, scared?" She forced a laugh and met Nick's eyes across the bed. "I wasn't scared. I knew you wouldn't leave me to go on the pack trips alone."

Harry glanced between them and nodded. "I want you to go with Nick."

"It was a joke, Harry," she said, careful to keep her tone light. "The pack trips aren't important."

Her uncle took hold of her arm with surprising force for a man who had been too weak to support himself earlier.

"I want you to promise me, Jenny. Promise me you won't cancel those pack trips. Promise me you'll take Nick with you. It's the only way to save the ranch."

She hesitated. A mixture of fear and dread pitted her stomach, but she couldn't upset her uncle while his heart was in such a precarious condition.

"I promise," she said.

Harry turned to Nick and raised his brow.

"I won't let anyone else touch her, sir."

Nick gave her uncle's shoulder a gentle squeeze, and Harry chuckled, seemingly satisfied.

Anyone *else*?

Jenny had no doubt Nick would protect her

from the other men, but who would protect her from him? She shot the dark-haired cowboy a warning look, which he sent straight back at her, along with his infamous grin—and suddenly she knew.

She was in serious trouble.

Five

NICK CURSED AS HE SHOOK HIS DEADENED thumb back to life. Couldn't he even hammer a stupid nail into a post? He needed to focus. Keep his mind off Jenny. He wasn't here to feel sorry for anyone. He needed the land, needed to figure out his next plan of action. Grasping the top of the wooden post for balance, he closed his eyes . . . and her face was closer than a coin toss away.

Her delicate brows arched upward when she was distressed. Her blue eyes darkened. Her lips parted ever so slightly. How could he think of anything else when she looked at him like that?

Jenny had been so vulnerable in the hospital waiting room. She'd needed him, needed his all-too-willing embrace.

He thought he'd finally made a connection with her, tasted the beginnings of friendship. But by the time they arrived back at the ranch that night, Jenny had become quiet, withdrawn, and once again completely beyond his reach.

The days had dragged into an unbearably long week. Each day he offered to go with Jenny to the hospital and each day she refused. Even worse was the fact that today, the day they were to bring Harry back home, she hadn't asked him to accompany her. She'd asked Wayne.

Despising himself and his inability to make Jenny develop any feelings for him, Nick dropped the wretched hammer he was using and trudged across the field to bring in the horses. The menacing black storm clouds were closing in fast and Jenny would have a fit if her beloved beasts were left out in the rain.

The first drops splattered the parched ground just as he reached the stable. Little Josh led two horses inside, but there were at least a dozen more that needed to come in, including Starfire and another of Jenny's favorites, a black and white Paint named Apache.

"Get your sorry tails over here," yelled

Frank, a halter and lead rope dangling from his hands.

The ranch hand was trying to separate Apache from the other geldings, but the lightning was scaring the horses into a wild frenzy.

"Need help?" Nick called, opening the paddock gate and letting himself in.

"Go that way," Frank instructed, "and try to head them toward me."

He went in the direction Frank indicated and began talking to the horses in a low soothing voice to coax them to stand still.

"Get behind them," Frank yelled, just as Josh reemerged from the stable. "Be careful, though. You have to whistle sharp when you go behind Apache. Make sure you whistle so he knows you're there."

Nick hesitated. "Won't a whistle spook him?"

"Nah. He's part deaf. Only a whistle will let the horse know you're behind him."

Nick knew it was standard practice to call out and touch the horse's backside as you circled around to let it know where you were, but a whistle? He couldn't remember hearing

Jenny whistle when she went by Apache's rear. But Frank knew more about these horses and their special quirks than he did, so he gave a sharp whistle as he approached.

All at once Apache's right hind leg shot straight out, caught him in the side, and sent him sprawling face first into the mud. For a moment all he saw was darkness. He wasn't even sure what had happened. Then he lifted his upper body off the ground and gasped as the searing pain in his ribs leveled him once again.

Spitting the gritty, manure-baked filth out of his mouth, he wiped his eyes just in time to see the devious smirk upon Frank's face.

"Oops! Sorry!"

Hooting with laughter, Frank slapped Josh on the back. Then, despite the growing storm, the two led the remaining horses into the stable without a single bit of trouble.

The intensifying rain drenched Nick's body and chilled his skin. The strong scent of hay and manure rose into his nostrils. He was as muddy as a stinking hog. He tried to move and once again the sting of the kick jarred into his side. Coughing between thrusts of rib-slicing pain, he brought himself up onto his hands and knees.

It was clear the ranch hands didn't want his friendship. Without Harry's presence on the ranch the mean-spirited pranks had escalated into daily rituals. They'd spilled paint into his black Stetson, greased his saddle, and rigged a bucket of water to splash over his head as he entered the barn. Now this.

The reality of his situation hit him full force. He wasn't any closer to obtaining Jenny's land than he was a week ago. The ranch hands hated him, the horses hated him, and Jenny had pretty much hated him ever since he'd initiated the bet.

Why couldn't he make her like him? He wasn't one to accept defeat easily, but he didn't think staying on at the ranch would accomplish anything. Trying to win Jenny's affection was like trying to cut cubes from a solid block of ice. It just wasn't worth the effort. If he couldn't melt her heart and get her land, so be it. He would just have to find another way to pay Billie's gambling debt.

❈   ❈   ❈

Jenny ran past Frank and sloshed through the ankle-deep mud of the paddock where Nick was on his hands and knees.

"Are you all right?" she asked, and pulled on his upper body in an attempt to lift him.

"*Ow!*" he shouted. "No, I'm not all right. What are you trying to do, finish me off?"

She dropped her hands and bit her lip as he struggled to his feet. "Apache was abused by his previous owner. He always back-kicks when he hears a whistle."

Nick winced, the pain evident on his face. "No kidding."

"Looks like the guys are giving you a hard time," she said, and reached out to steady him.

"Not half as hard as you."

A twinge of guilt twisted her gut. She'd been hostile toward the man ever since his arrival despite his hard work and much-needed ranching skills. Then, after helping her transport Harry to the hospital, she'd avoided him.

She'd wanted to break free of the invisible pull he had on her and distance herself from him. But now, as they stood face-to-face, she realized she hadn't distanced herself from anything. Here he was, in all his dynamic glory, covered with mud, spiteful and angry, and she was drawn to him even more than before.

"I want to help you," she shouted over the rumbling thunder.

"Leave?"

"No," she said, smiling at his bitterness, "with Harry laid up I have no choice but to keep you here."

"You don't need me," he said, the mud streaking down his handsome face. "Frank's made it clear he intends to run the ranch himself, and I'm sure Wayne will accompany you on the pack trip next weekend."

"What are you saying?"

"You win. I'm packing my bags."

"No! You can't leave."

"Why?" he demanded.

"Because I—I want you to stay."

He gave her a swift, startled look so intense it made her take a step backward. Catching her hand, he began slowly reeling her back in.

"Why?" he asked again, his tone becoming soft, luring, and far more intimidating.

"I . . ." She wished he'd let go of her. She wished she could slip away. Squirming like a trout caught on the end of a fishing line, her mind darted to and fro desperately searching for a way off the hook. "W-we've got to get in out of the rain," she stammered.

"Not until you answer my question." He drew her closer. "Why do you want me to stay?"

"There are a lot of reasons. You work hard. You ride well. Harry likes you . . ."

Nick let out a disgruntled laugh, and gave her a direct look that said he was plainly unconvinced.

"Give me a real reason."

Lightning flashed, thunder boomed, and the rain drove down in torrents. The ground shook, threatening to split apart the very foundation she stood on.

"It wouldn't kill you to admit *you* like me," he said, baiting her.

"All right. Fine," she spat angrily. "I like you. Is that what you wanted to hear?"

"Yes," he said with a grin, "very much."

The way he looked at her made her pulse race nearly as fast as the beat of the driving rain that poured down over them. Then he tugged on her hand and nodded toward the shelter of the dry buildings.

"Can you make it up to the house?" she asked.

"I hope so," Nick replied. He winced with each step, but at least he could walk.

"I'll be there in a few minutes," she said, and clenched her hands into fists as the faint strains of chortled laughter met her ears. "There's just one more thing I need to do."

❖   ❖   ❖

JENNY ENTERED THE STABLE, THE NEWEST BUILDING on the ranch, and wiped her face with a nearby towel. "Frank, you're fired."

The ranch hands were gathered around Wayne, who had missed the outdoor excitement—and as they turned to look at her, their laughter dropped off into stunned silence.

"Hey, look, I was doing you a favor," said Frank, puffing out his chest. "Chandler's no ranch manager and you know it. He just came here to win the bet. What you need is a real man."

"A real man?" she retorted. "While you and your friends are off playing cards, drinking beer, and wasting time on stupid pranks, Nick Chandler has been working his butt off!

219

Do you think I haven't noticed who brings the cows in at night or who's been harvesting the hay? Why, he puts every single one of you to shame."

"You fool!" Frank exclaimed, his face aghast. "You're falling right into his trap."

Jenny pointed to the door. "You can pack your gear and leave."

Wayne and little Josh stood frozen, staring openmouthed as if afraid she'd fire them next.

Jenny turned to Wayne and his face paled. "While Chandler and I are away on the pack trips, you will be in charge of the ranch."

"Me?" Wayne relaxed his stance and smiled at Frank's glowering face. "I guess I can be a real man from time to time."

Realizing Frank hadn't moved, Jenny gave him a little wave. "Goodbye, Frank."

"I'll get you back for this," Frank promised as he stomped away. "You just watch and see."

Jenny pushed aside Frank's threat of revenge as she climbed the stairs of the old two-story timber house. She would worry about him later. Right now, her main concern was if any of Nick's bones had been broken. She stepped through the doorway of his room to find him struggling, without much success, to remove the wet T-shirt from his upper body.

"Here, let me," she said, setting her black medical bag on the table and moving forward to help him.

"I'm okay. It's just a little—" He drew in a sharp breath as she pulled the dripping garment up over his head.

"Sore?" she asked, and slung the shirt over the back of a chair.

"Yes."

"Are there any sharp, knifelike pains?"

"I don't . . . think so," he replied, his voice ragged.

Her gaze drifted over his bare shoulders, down his finely toned chest, and finally focused on the place along his rib cage she was supposed to be examining.

"Oh, my gosh!" she exclaimed, staring at the horrendous purplish black bruise on his left side.

"It's not as bad as it looks."

"To make sure there's nothing broken, I'm going to have to press on it."

She stared at the wound, her fingers hovering in midair just a mere inch away from his skin.

"Afraid to touch me?" he teased.

"No," she said, and pressed against his rib cage.

He flinched. "*Oww! Blast it all to—*"

"Sorry," she apologized.

"I'm not sure who is worse," he said, clenching his teeth, "you or Frank."

"I fired Frank," she said without looking up.

"You did?"

"Of course, I did. You could have been killed." She dug in her black medical bag and brought out a roll of white bandaging tape. "I don't think anything is broken, but I'm going to wrap your ribs anyway."

As she circled his upper body, an acute sense of awareness shortened her breath and made her fingers tremble. While working on the ranch she'd seen plenty of men without their shirts, but Nick's upper torso was, well . . . superb, and she was so darn close to it.

"Anyone less . . . muscled," she said, swallowing hard, "could have been seriously hurt. Still, it's probably too painful for you to ride."

"I can ride," he said, giving her a dark look. "Don't you dare try to use this as an excuse to leave me behind on the pack trips."

"But the first pack trip is next weekend. That's just six days from now. You can't possibly . . ."

"You promised Harry you'd take me with you."

"That was before you got hurt."

"I'll be fine. Besides, I thought you enjoyed finding new ways to torture me."

"Absolutely," she said, smiling.

Suddenly, the power went out and a loud clap of thunder shook the darkened room.

"Stay here with me," he said, hooking an arm around her waist and drawing her toward him, "and you can torture me all you like."

"Forget it, cowboy." She pulled away from his grasp and gathered her medical supplies. At the doorway she hesitated and glanced back at him over her shoulder. "Just because I like you doesn't mean I want to jump into bed with you," she warned. "I still intend to win the bet."

Nick gave her one of his sly heart-stopping grins. "Me too."

Jenny stared at the phone in her father's office, each unanswered ring twisting her stomach in knots. Just another creditor demanding to know when they'd get their money. How could she speak to them when she didn't have any answers?

She still needed to pay Harry's hospital bill. The insurance didn't cover much, and the doctor's fee was higher than she'd expected. Perhaps if she had stayed in medical school and become a doctor, she wouldn't have a pile of unpaid invoices on her desk.

Jenny ripped open the top envelope and discovered another offer from N.L.C. Industries to buy her property. She was just about to toss it into the trash when she stopped to see the monetary figure they had in mind. Not enough, she thought as she tore it in two. It would never be enough to make her give up the land she loved.

Frustrated, Jenny left the room and made her way down to the stable.

"Hey, big boy." She leaned over the half-door of Starfire's stall and patted his sleek brown neck. "Who's the most handsome fella in the whole barn? You are, aren't you? Yes, you are."

"I'd give anything to have you talk to me like that."

Recognizing the voice, she spun around, and a surge of excitement raced around inside her at the sight of Nick's smiling face. Nick hadn't been outside much since his injury. Why, it had been downright *dull* working on the ranch this past week without him there to trail after her, tease her, and tempt her to think . . . traitorous thoughts.

Nick gave her a searching look. "Did you miss me?"

Why did he always have to be so darn direct? If she said yes, it would reveal too much, and if she said no, he'd know she was lying.

"We all missed you," she said. "The chores have backed up and there's a lot to do around here."

"Is that all I am to you, another pair of hands? You could tell me I'm handsome to make me feel better."

Suddenly, a forceful nudge broke them apart, and Starfire nibbled her cheek.

Nick arched his brow. "Somebody's jealous."

"No," Jenny said, smiling. "Just hungry. Can the second most handsome fella in the barn help me feed the horses?"

Nick grinned. "Only if you'll tell me how to become your number one."

Never leave. Jenny gazed into his eyes but couldn't say the words. Instead she shrugged. "Well, Starfire is a hard guy to beat."

Six

NICK STUFFED AN EXTRA SHIRT INTO HIS backpack as Billie entered his bedroom and closed the door.

"Did you search Jenny's room?" he asked, adding a pair of pants to the pack as well.

"Mission accomplished." Billie flopped down on the end of his bed. "First off, she isn't the neatest person you've met. Clothes are tossed everywhere, old bridles hang in her closet, and every flat surface is covered with family photographs."

"Sounds a lot like her tack room," he mused. "Did you find anything useful?"

"She likes men in white dress shirts. It was written in her journal. She thinks white dress shirts are sexy."

"Slim chance of wearing a white dress shirt on a ranch. Anything else?"

"She likes to read." Billie tossed a book into his lap. "Romances. Her shelves are lined with them."

Nick studied the book cover. A man and a woman were dancing in a rose garden. "How do the men in the books make the women fall in love with them?"

"How should I know?" said Billie, throwing her hands up in the air. "*I* certainly don't read them. But maybe you should. The men have arrived for the pack trips and are flirting with her like mad."

"They're here?" Nick crossed to the window and sucked in his breath. Almost a dozen men surrounded Jenny in the yard below. "They think they can win the bet and search for the gold at the same time."

"Good luck," said Billie.

Her woeful tone reminded him of the uphill battle he was about to face. With so many others vying for Jenny's attention, when would he have a moment alone with her?

❖   ❖   ❖

JENNY LINED UP THE PACK STRING AND MADE SOME last-minute adjustments in the pecking order.

Most designated wilderness areas in Washington limited the party size of humans and animals to a combination of twelve heartbeats, but she would be taking her group into the Lake Chelan-Sawtooth Wilderness, which allowed twelve people plus eighteen pack and saddle animals. Her stomach twisted in knots just thinking about it. She was going to be up in the mountains, alone, with eleven men.

Even now, the thought of backing out crossed her mind, but she was the only one who knew the trails, could cook, *and* had medical experience in case of an emergency.

"Trust Nick," Harry said, and handed her a coil of rope. "He won't let any of those men touch you."

"How can you be so sure?"

"Oh, I'm sure." Her uncle chuckled.

"And if Nick should misbehave?"

"He won't," Harry assured her. "But it wouldn't hurt to let him get to know you, Jenny. If you are ever going to love someone, you're going to have to take risks."

Heat rose into her cheeks. "I am not going to risk loving a man who only wants to win a bet."

Her uneasiness grew as Charlie Pickett,

David Wilson, and Kevin Forester arrived. Hadn't she told those three seasoned cowboys she didn't want to marry them?

Charlie inherited his ranch from his grand-father, but he dreamed of singing and one day becoming a recording artist with platinum music awards displayed on his wall. He wasn't committed to Pine, and she suspected he might leave if offered a contract to go on tour.

David was quiet, a bit untidy in appearance, and his best friend was a hound dog who liked to drool all over the front porch. While she ap-preciated his sincerity and ability to live off the land like his grandpa, Levi MacGowan, he didn't appear quick-witted and he lacked ambition.

Kevin owned a ranch three tracts over, on the other side of the Hansons' hayfields. He shared a love of horses, something she could relate to, but he was also a fireman whose heart had been burned by his last girlfriend. Pas-sion didn't extend past his cowboy poetry, and Jenny knew he proposed only as a friend.

Ted Andrews, owner of Andrew's Auto Garage, had also laid down money at the café, but he was so obnoxious his bet didn't count. The man couldn't even ranch.

Her hands trembled as she checked off their names on her clipboard and collected their money. She should have gone over the sign-up sheet herself instead of letting Harry do it, but after coming home from the hospital her uncle needed a task to make him feel useful.

"Jenny!" Wayne hurried toward her with his hand locked on Billie's arm. "Shouldn't she be going with you? What if she has an epileptic seizure?"

Billie yanked her arm free and screwed her face into an infuriated scowl. "I am *not* epileptic."

"We're only allowed twelve people," Jenny told him. She smiled at Billie. "And she's not epileptic."

"That's not what she said when she came here," Wayne argued. "I heard she was epileptic and had nightmares."

"The only nightmare around here is you," Billie shouted, and kicked him in the shin.

Jenny laughed and patted Wayne's arm. "Take her into town for a drink and she'll be fine."

Out of the corner of her eye, she spied an old man with a long white ponytail tying a

231

weathered green rucksack behind the saddle of one of the packhorses.

"Levi, what on earth are *you* doing here?"

"Goin' on a pack trip," he said, brushing down his white woolly whiskers.

"But—" Jenny's mind whirled. "You've been exploring these mountains since before I was born. Why would you want to pay *me* to take you on a pack trip?"

"For the entertainment," he said, his eyes twinkling. "Never in the history of Pine has there been a more anticipated event, and you can be darn sure I ain't gonna miss it."

"I'm afraid you might be disappointed," she told him. "We're just going to ride up Wild Bear Ridge, camp, and ride back down again. You've already done that a thousand times."

"Yep," he said with a chuckle, "but never with a group of eleven men who are all tryin' to marry one woman. It should prove to be *mighty* interesting."

She tried to laugh. She wanted to cry. She glanced at Nick, who was loading sleeping bags and tents into the pack boxes, and her tension eased.

Despite her initial protests, she was glad the

tall, dark-haired cowboy was coming along. No matter how bleak the situation, his lighthearted banter could always make her smile.

Except he didn't banter with her as they headed out over the old logging trail. He didn't even ride next to her. While she rode in front of the group, Nick brought up the rear to make sure no one fell behind.

"Quite a view," sang Charlie Pickett, riding up beside her as they crested the rocky bluff at Talon's Point, "but not half so pretty as you."

She attempted a smile, and failed, wishing she could escape and fly like the eagles circling above.

She should be happy. It was a perfect day for the pack trip. A light breeze held off the summer heat. The scent of the lush green meadow grass was remarkably fragrant. And the day was filled with sparkling sunshine. Who couldn't be happy when the sun was shining?

Me, Jenny thought, chewing on a sprig of fresh mint. She'd been hearing corny comments all morning as each of the men vied to ride in the position beside her on the trail. Each of the men, that is, except Nick. He remained a million miles away at the tail end of the pack string.

By mid-afternoon, she stopped the group at the twenty-five-foot fire tower, where they would camp for the night. Following her lead, the men dismounted, tied the horses to the hitching rail, and climbed the two flights of creaky stairs to the top. The glass windows of the timber cabin were dusty, so they went out to the wrap-around deck to get a better look at the land below.

"Wild Bear Lookout was built in nineteen thirty-eight and manned by the U.S. forest service until nineteen ninety-seven," she said, gazing at the town of Pine and the surrounding ranches miles below. "It's been abandoned ever since."

"Great place to see fireworks," Ted Andrews commented, "although I see fireworks every time I look at you, Jenny."

She rolled her eyes in disgust and the men laughed.

"Fireworks have been banned this year. The area is too dry," Kevin informed them, "but, Jenny, look!"

Kevin pointed into the sky. Red smoke billowed out in streams behind a single-engine plane maneuvering a dancelike formation across the sky.

"What in tarnation is that there fella tryin' to do?" Levi exclaimed.

"He's writing a message," Kevin told them. "The pilot is a friend of mine."

"I see some letters forming now," said Charlie. Then he began to sing, "It says . . . 'Jenny marry me?'"

"The pilot wants to marry Jenny?" asked David, scratching his scruffy brown head.

"No, you imbecile. *I do.* I paid the pilot to write the message for *me*." Grabbing hold of her waist from behind, Kevin pulled her close. "Jenny, we've known each other since grade school and I figure marriage is a practical solution to both our problems. I have no money to loan you, but if you marry me, I'd be happy to sell my ranch to save yours. I need the river to water my herds, and to me, a marriage between us just makes sense. So what do you say?"

Her stomach locked down hard. If she *were* to marry, she didn't want a marriage that just made sense. She wanted what her parents had—true love.

"Sorry, Kevin." She twisted out of his arms and darted away from him, her heart pounding.

Kevin frowned. "I've been denied."

Of course he was denied. She would deny every single one of them. Kneeling, Jenny squeezed the handle of her boot knife, and let the air exhale out of her lungs. If Kevin had held her a moment longer, she might have used the knife to protect herself. Especially since it appeared her appointed bodyguard wasn't going to intervene.

She glanced at Nick, who hovered toward the back of the group. He watched her, but neither smiled nor said a word. What was wrong with him? Didn't he care Kevin had his arms around her?

Jenny drew closer to him to find out. She put eight of the horses into the preexisting ten-by-ten wooden corrals. The rest were tied to high hitch-lines, which Nick set up between the trees.

"How's it going?" he asked, his focus on the leftover rope he was coiling.

"Well, the men are having fun. Except for the incident with Kevin Forester at the top of the fire tower, and the other with Charlie Pickett down below, the pack trip appears to be a success. What do you think?"

"I'm starving," he said, finally meeting her gaze. "When are you going to cook?"

"Is food the *only* thing on your mind?"

Nick nodded, his expression innocent. "Yes."

Stunned, Jenny watched the handsome dark-haired cowboy shift his attention back to the rope.

Why was he so quiet? Why didn't he smile or flirt with her like usual? She shot him a look of annoyance and stumbled over a root on her way to unload the cooking supplies.

❖ ❖ ❖

NICK GRINNED BEHIND HER BACK. THE MEN WERE IN rare form this day, and she was going to need him to step in and save her before the night was over.

Listening to all their conceit and murmured intentions had aggravated him to no end. The skywriting proposal had been especially irritating. Why hadn't *he* thought of something like that?

But what riled his temper the most was

when Charlie Pickett tried to carry Jenny into the remote ground-level equipment garage that lay fifty feet from the base of the fire tower. Fortunately, the garage door had been locked, and with a sheepish grin the music-loving cowboy set her back down on her feet.

He'd given Charlie a new song to sing when the others weren't looking, and by the time the guy returned to the fire tower, he was sporting a purplish blaze of color around his right eye.

Yes, she was going to need him to save her tonight, but not until she really needed it. All the other men who wrangled for her attention were making him look good. Perhaps later tonight, after they'd become more obnoxious, he would look even better.

She admitted she liked him, and from the way she kept sneaking peeks back at him while on the trail, he couldn't help but hope she'd start to show him some affection.

It would take some control on his part to restrain himself, but the longer he waited before stepping in to rescue her, the more appreciative she would be when he did. He just had to hold off for the right moment.

❖　　❖　　❖

JENNY STIRRED THE HAMBURGER, BEANS, ONIONS, and tomatoes into a thick, spicy chili sauce. The smell encouraged the men to build a campfire in the metal ring next to the picnic table.

As soon as the coals were ready, she set in three cast-iron Dutch oven kettles stacked on top of each other. The chili simmered in the large bottom kettle, biscuits baked in the medium-sized middle kettle, and the apple cobbler she'd made for dessert cooked in the small kettle on top. The heat traveling up the towering cast-iron trio cooked each entry to perfection, and the men devoured the food as if they hadn't eaten in days.

"The way to a man's heart is good cooking—and, Jenny, my dear, this is *good* cooking," Ted Andrews informed her.

"Whose tent will *you* be sleeping in, Jenny?" asked Charlie, passing around a flask of whiskey. "There's plenty of room in mine."

"I sleep alone," she assured him, and then frowned. "Charlie, how did you get a black eye?"

"A low-hanging branch caught me by surprise near the fire tower," he said, and shot Nick a swift glance.

Jenny gave Nick a questioning look but he

only shrugged and turned away to open a bag of marshmallows.

"Charlie, I can't allow alcohol to be a part of my pack trips. You'll have to put the liquor away."

"He'll put it away, all right," Ted Andrews interjected, "in his stomach. Hey, Charlie, give me some."

"I said no alcohol," she insisted.

"You can't expect a man not to indulge in a little drink while out in the wild," said Levi MacGowan, taking out his own flask. "It jus' wouldn't be natural."

It would affect their brains and make them even more eager to lay their hands on her. She looked to Nick for help, but to her utter frustration, he smiled and took a sip from the flask Levi offered him.

Drat. Levi was like a grandfather to her. And he loved his home-brewed whiskey. She didn't have the heart, *or the nerve*, to forbid him to drink after he'd paid to come on a pack trip he didn't need her to lead. And if she couldn't forbid Levi to drink, she couldn't forbid the others.

As the night wore on, the men edged closer,

like a howling band of coyotes moving in on their prey. She couldn't even go to the pit toilet without one of the men trying to follow her. What on earth was she going to do?

Levi MacGowan sat wide-eyed around the fire as he took it all in. Nick, however, acted as if he didn't even notice.

"In case you have forgotten," she said, marching toward him, "you promised Harry you would protect me on this trip."

"You're a tough gal," Nick said with a shrug. "If anyone gets out of control, just slap him as hard as you slapped me that first day in the café."

She stared at him in disbelief. A mere slap was not going to stop this drunken band of perverts. Surely, he could see that. What did he want her to do? Beg for his help?

She was trying to return to her seat on the opposite side of the campfire when Kevin Forester reached out a big looping arm and pulled her on to his lap.

"I've got a warm seat right here for you, honey," he bellowed.

"Oh, no you don't," said Ted Andrews, tugging her away from the campfire and into the encircling shadows. "The little lady is mine."

"Let her go," said David Wilson, and he reached out to draw her back into the edge of firelight. "If she's gonna be with anyone, it's gonna be *me*."

"Why, you little bushy-haired punk!" Ted exclaimed, giving David a shove.

Kevin and Charlie stood in David's defense, and suddenly Jenny found herself in the middle of a brawl.

She bent low to dodge the flurry of flying fists and pulled out her boot knife. Her protection. The one reliable thing she could always count on to keep her safe.

But before she could use it, someone whisked the knife out of her hands and fired a deafening shot into the clear mountain air.

"I'd appreciate it, men," said Nick, his hand on his rifle, "if you would keep your hands *off* my fiancée."

Nick's deadly tone, filled with more fury than she had ever thought possible, was enough to momentarily freeze everyone in their tracks.

"Come here," he commanded, crooking his finger at her.

She moved to obey, her limbs trembling,

and gave him a cautious look as she reached his side.

"I must be hearing things," Ted Andrews exclaimed, narrowing his eyes on Nick. "What did you just say?"

"He called her his *fiancée*," David informed him.

All at once the men loosened up and started to laugh.

Kevin slapped his thigh. "Good one, Chandler."

Nick clicked the rifle into ready position and fixed each man with a hard stare. "I'm not joking."

"You can't possibly expect us to believe she's going to marry *you*," Ted exclaimed. "Hell would freeze over before she'd ever marry *you*."

"Yeah," Charlie Pickett added, "what about the bet?"

"Ask her," Nick challenged.

"*Are* you his fiancée?" asked Ted.

Her breath caught in her throat as all eyes turned toward her, including Nick's. If she said no, the men would feel free to attack her. If she lied and said yes, it was possible they might leave her alone. She hesitated only a moment.

243

"Yes," she said, struggling to control her quavering voice, "I am Nick's fiancée."

Levi MacGowan's wrinkled blue eyes popped with excitement. Nick shot her a quick grin, handed her back her boot knife, and took a seat on a big overturned log.

"I still don't believe it," said Ted with rising hostility. "If they are really engaged, then I want to see her kiss him."

"Yeah," Kevin shouted. "Convince us, Jenny. Kiss him."

"What?" she sputtered.

"It wouldn't kill you," Nick said in a low voice only she could hear.

Her cheeks blazed with heat. Of course, it wouldn't kill her. What was one kiss, anyway? It was simply the lesser of two evils. With one kiss she could stop the entire group from pursuing her. She met Nick's expectant gaze with uncertainty.

Drat! Taking a deep breath, she approached the log he was sitting on and placed a terrified hand on each of his shoulders. It was only a kiss, she reminded herself shakily. She wasn't selling her soul.

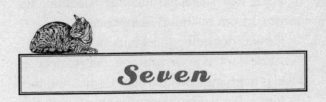

Seven

NICK SCARCELY DARED TO BREATHE AS JENNY drew toward him, bent her head, and brushed her sweet, whisper-soft lips against his.

It was the simplest of gestures, yet the kiss, freely given, set off an assortment of emotional charges he'd never expected.

Longing. He hadn't realized until now how much he'd longed for this moment.

Adoration. He wasn't sure if it was the helpless expression in her eyes as she walked toward him or her spitfire resolve to see the deed through, but he adored her.

Fear. He'd never felt this way before. His heart pounded with the erratic hoofbeats of a stampede gone berserk, yet his body remained paralyzed. Gone was the ability to use his arms or legs. Or his brain.

What had she done to him? All thoughts vanished from his mind except one.

He was not going to let her go.

As he slanted his mouth over hers to deepen the kiss her hands pushed against his shoulder.

Please, Jenny. The silent cry echoed between them as he moved his mouth back and forth over hers. *Kiss me.*

When she did, the wave of exhilaration that washed over him was so powerful, it nearly knocked him backward.

She tasted like a sprig of fresh mint. Invigoratingly fresh. Adrenaline-pumping fresh. Inspiring, soaring, top-of-the world fresh.

Terrified she'd pull away, he cupped the back of her head with his hand to hold her in place. This time she didn't protest, but leaned in even closer. Close enough for her hair to touch his cheek and alter all perception of reality.

Time passed unnoticed, and when they finally drew apart, Jenny whispered, "Was that convincing?"

"You convinced *me.*"

His goal was to win Jenny's heart, not lose his own. Still, it didn't hurt to desire the woman you planned to marry. It would make winning the bet that much sweeter.

"Are they still watching?" she asked.

He looked behind her at the empty seats beside the dying embers of the fire, and smiled.

"Yes," he lied. "You better kiss me again."

❖   ❖   ❖

DREAMS HALF FORGOTTEN REKINDLED IN THE BACK of Jenny's mind as Nick illuminated the fire tower with a flashlight, and led her up the tall flight of creaking stairs.

She no longer cared about being the only woman on the pack trip. The warm air was fluttering softly around her, the sky overhead was speckled with an extraordinary array of stars, and Nick was by her side.

He took her in his arms and bent his head to invite her to his kiss. She didn't need much coaxing. One of his grins followed by a glittering mischievous look melted her heart like liquid paraffin.

Was it just her or was the air growing warmer and more intense? The light breeze had indeed kicked up a notch and whistled as it whipped around them, making the fire tower tremble. The wind didn't bother her, though. She could have withstood a hurricane as long as Nick continued to kiss her like this. Like she was the only woman he'd ever wanted.

He kissed her long and slow until her head began to spin and bells began to ring in her ears. Not bells. She broke her lips away from his. Sirens.

Nick must have heard it, too, for he turned to look out over the fire tower balcony. Jenny drew in a sharp breath. An orange blaze, chased by the wind, barreled down the mountainside.

"It's headed toward the ranch," she exclaimed, terror squelching all other emotions as she raced down the fire tower steps. "There's a forest service road that leads straight down the mountain. If we ride fast, we can be at the ranch in less than an hour."

Rousting the others from their tents, they left the camp equipment behind and mounted the horses. Jenny squeezed Starfire's reins so tight she lost feeling in her fingers. She had to remind herself to breathe. To hope. If anything were to happen to the ranch now, she didn't know what she would do.

❁   ❁   ❁

THEY HADN'T BEEN RIDING TWENTY MINUTES WHEN they came face to face with a wall of fire. Heat filled the forest, turning it into an oven. Pine needles sizzled and smoke suffocated the air. The horses whinnied and a few began to buck and rear.

Jenny gripped the front edge of her saddle, her heart pounding. "The road is completely blocked," she warned. "We'll have to take the path to the left through the trees."

Jenny's great-great grandfather had named the ranch Windy Meadows because it was in a valley between Sasquatch Spire and Mount MacGowan. The wind tunneled through, like a natural air-conditioner to keep them cool in summer, but with the fury of a blowtorch during forest fires.

The journey down the mountain seemed to take forever. They finally came out alongside Charlie Pickett's property.

"His back fields are already in flames," Jenny shouted. "It's only a matter of minutes before it reaches—"

She couldn't finish the sentence. Windy

Meadows couldn't burn, not after all her efforts to save it. Perhaps if they all worked fast enough they could divert the flames.

Jenny dismounted her horse and ran down the path to the corral, where the fire raced to meet her.

Harry, who shouldn't have been standing, barked directions to Wayne, who began to dig a dirt trench around the outlying buildings. Billie wet down the roof of the hay barn with the garden hose and filled buckets from the outdoor faucet.

Would it be enough? As Nick hurried out to the field to join the men, Jenny ran toward the stable. She had six horses that hadn't gone on the pack trip left inside.

A reverberating neigh pierced her ears and was joined by several loud crashes and thuds as she crossed the threshold of the open door. She grabbed a halter and lead rope off the hook on the wall and headed for the first stall, where Apache was trying to kick the walls apart.

"Easy, boy," she said, strapping the halter around his black-and-white head and running her hand along the side of his neck. "Let's get you out of here."

Jenny led the frightened horse out the door and with a slap on his rump, sent him running off down the trail to the safety of the open pasture opposite the ranch.

A fire truck arrived, its sirens blaring as it drove past her on its way down to the fields. Kevin ran forward to suit up and join his firefighter friends. Three pickup trucks followed. She paused and watched as a dozen men she knew from town, all carrying shovels and pickaxes, jumped from the backs of the trucks ready to lend a hand.

She hoped her uncle wouldn't try to help. He wasn't strong enough to be fighting fires.

A plane flew overhead, dropping gallons of water from the air as she turned to go back through the stable door.

Smoke filled the corridor, and Jenny hurried to Echo's stall. The mare snorted, almost stepping on her as she unlatched the door.

"Go on," Jenny urged.

Pushing past her, Echo bolted out the stable entrance.

She rushed to the next stall and jumped backward as a large beam crashed down from the ceiling. Scorching flames shot in all directions, igniting the wooden interior of the building and sending the horses into a frenzied panic.

Time was running out.

Jenny unlatched the sliding locks to every stall door. One horse raced to freedom, while three others, terrified by the sight of the fire, were unable to leave.

Kastle was one of them. The beautiful gray mare was rearing up and tossing its head, its eyes wide.

If only she had a bandanna, or a towel, to use as a blindfold. Searching the corridor for any scrap of cloth that might work, Jenny spotted an empty horse treat bag on the ground just twenty feet away.

She was about to retrieve it when an explosion knocked her to the ground amid an avalanche of sparks. Timber rained down from the roof. If she could just make it to her feet . . .

Struggling to free herself from the debris, she glanced up for just a second and screamed at the top of her lungs.

A falling beam was headed straight toward her.

❖   ❖   ❖

NICK SHIELDED HIS EYES FROM THE SEARING HEAT as Kevin Forester pulled him away from the fire line he and the other men were digging.

"Without the wind we'd have a chance," Kevin yelled, "but it's blowing the fire out of control. We have to get out of here while we still can."

Nick nodded. Three air tankers and two helicopters circled above, dropping water and retardant on the flames, but still the fire advanced from every direction.

Another blast shook the ground as the tractor shed exploded and splintering fragments of wood shot skyward.

"My drums of gasoline!" Harry shouted, throwing his arms up into the air.

Spotting Wayne through the smoke a few feet ahead of him, Nick grabbed the back of the ranch hand's shirt.

"Where's Jenny?"

"In the stable," Wayne said, pointing.

The entire structure was engulfed in flames and half of the roof had already collapsed.

"Please, Lord," said Nick, taking off on a dead run, "let her be safe."

He entered through the side door and

looked down the main corridor but couldn't see her. His heart lurched in his chest.

"Jenny!" Raising his voice, he called out again. *"Jenny!"*

"Over here."

He followed the sound of her voice and found her inside one of the end stalls.

"My leg is trapped," she said, wincing as she tried to move.

"Don't worry, I've got you."

He pulled off the tangle of beams, but when Jenny tried to stand, her leg gave out beneath her.

"Kastle won't leave her stall," she said, trying to crawl toward the terrified horse. "I have to get her out of here."

"I've got to get *you* out of here first," Nick said, scooping her up in his arms. He was making his way down the aisle when a large figure stepped into the doorway, blocking the exit.

"Frank, what are you doing here?" Jenny exclaimed.

"I told you I'd get you back," the former ranch hand said with a malicious glint in his eyes. "You fired the wrong man, missy. Nice little joke, isn't it? You fired me, and now I am *fire*-ing you."

Nick glanced at the axe gripped tightly in Frank's hands. *He meant to kill them.*

"You set the fire?" asked Jenny, her gaze also on the weapon.

"Of course, I did," boasted Frank, raising the axe above his head.

"You won't get away with it," Nick growled.

"Oh, yeah? And who is going to stop me? You? The CEO of N.L.C. Industries?"

Nick gasped, and a ball of dread ripped a hole through his gut, making him feel hollow. Jenny's body went rigid in his arms.

"Oh, yeah, I know your little secret." Frank chuckled, clearly enjoying the moment. "You left one too many bags of cookies lying around the stable. Jenny, did you know Fat Happy Horse Treats was a manufactured product of N.L.C. Industries?"

Nick glanced at Jenny's horrified expression.

"I guess not," Frank said with a grin. "Sorry to spill the beans, Nick."

"The *CEO* of . . . No, you're wrong." Jenny shook her head. "He can't be . . ."

"His full name is Nicholas Lawrence Chandler," Frank informed her.

Jenny jerked around and looked straight into his eyes.

The truth must have been written all over his face, because in the next instant she tried to pull away from him. He continued to hold her tight. "I'll explain later."

"Explain? What is there to explain?"

"I also know about the little scheme you have with my cousin, the bank manager," Frank added.

"What scheme?" Jenny asked, her voice barely audible over the crackling fire.

"He's trying to romance the land away from you so he can sell it to Stewart Davenport along with his own three parcels. Davenport won't buy his land without yours." Frank drew back the axe, ready to strike. "Now no one will have it."

The axe swung toward them like a pendulum on a clock ready to ring their death chime. With Jenny in his arms, Nick leapt to the side, escaping a narrow miss. The axe buried itself into the large wooden support post next to him instead.

A thunderous explosion sounded above.

Jenny clung to him, her fingernails digging into the back of his neck, as the roof above the beam began to collapse. Nick tried to shield Jenny from the raining debris and used his quick reflexes to dodge the impending onslaught.

Frank, however, was lit up as bright as the noonday sun. The big man's eyes darted to and fro as the flames raced over his body. But instead of dropping to the ground and rolling, he screamed and ran out the door.

Nick ran after him, with Jenny in his arms, but it was too late. Frank's life was drawn away by the flames right before their eyes.

Two firefighters covered Frank with a blanket and radioed for help as Nick set Jenny on the ground.

"I'll be right back," he promised.

"Where are you going?"

"I've got to get the horses out," Nick said, and turned back toward the stable.

❧   ❧   ❧

JENNY SAT ON THE GROUND STARING WITH DISBELIEF at what was going on around her. Could this really be happening? It all seemed so unreal, like a scene out of a movie.

Despite the scorching heat, her entire body trembled. She strained to see through the thick smoke surrounding the stable. Two more horses ran out the door but still no sign of Nick. She was tempted to go after him, but she wouldn't get far with the sprained ankle.

She glanced at Kevin, dressed in his firefighter suit, as he and another fireman carried Frank's charred body away on a stretcher.

"Are you okay?" cried Billie, running toward her. "Where's Nick?"

She pointed toward the stable. "He's trying to save the horses."

"The whole thing is an inferno!"

Jenny wrapped her arms around her middle and rocked back and forth, her throat dry with the taste of burnt embers. The sight of the flames transported her back six months before when the old barn had caught fire. Déjà vu disoriented her. Would her father come out? No, her father had died. He'd died in the barn. This wasn't the barn. This was the stable. Would Nick come out?

Harry walked toward her, a large black smudge on his cheek. "Wayne has the truck running. We have to go *now*."

"My brother is in the stable," Billie squealed, her voice shrill.

Jenny fixed her eyes on the entrance. She waited five minutes . . . ten . . .

Wayne joined them, wondering what was taking so long, why they couldn't leave.

Suddenly a large gray mass burst through the flames and she tried to jump to her feet, forgetting until the last moment that her leg was injured. Biting back the stinging pain, she hopped up and down with her weight on one foot and leaned against Billie. Together they stepped forward, anxiously holding their breath.

It's him! Jenny could hardly contain herself as Nick's unmistakable outline emerged from the thick smoke. He was running beside Kastle, with the burlap horse treat bag over the feisty mare's head.

Billie ran forward to meet him and he gave his sister a quick squeeze. Then he turned and looked at *her*, his eyes dark with uncertainty, and the present world resumed with amazing focus.

A flaming arrow of searing pain shot through her heart, leaving her breathless, leaving her numb.

"Nick Chandler is the CEO of N.L.C. Industries," she told Harry and Wayne. "I never knew Nick's middle name. Never put it together. *Nicholas Lawrence Chandler–N.L.C.*"

"What!" Wayne demanded. He looked from Nick to Billie.

Harry shut his mouth up tight. What did he think of his choice for a ranch manager now?

Jenny's thoughts turned toward her devious *bank* manager. Stewart Davenport probably thought he couldn't lose. It was a well-known fact he used his bank position for personal gain. He wanted her property for himself and if she didn't foreclose, he'd get Nick to romance the ranch away from her. She'd almost fallen for it.

She started to turn toward the waiting trucks when Nick sprinted to her side.

"Jenny, wait," Nick pleaded, grabbing hold of her arm. "Let me explain. Since I met you, all of my original plans have changed." Nick's voice was raw, heartfelt, convincing until he added, *"Trust me."*

Trust him? When he'd kept the fact he was the *CEO of N.L.C. Industries*—the one sending her all the proposals to buy her land—a secret from her? She stared at him and in the back of her mind all she saw was Travis.

"I . . ." She swallowed hard and the horrible suspicion she'd once again been duped by a man who claimed to care about her pushed its way to the center of her thoughts.

"Trust me," Nick repeated in a whisper.

She saw the tension in his face, the desperation in his eyes, but shook her head. "I *can't*."

Nick's face paled and a muscle jumped along the side of his jaw. He opened his mouth as if to say something more, but the firefighters needed his help and he left.

Jenny's heart begged to run after him, yet her feet remained glued with firm refusal. She had too many questions, too many suspicions.

Had Nick been faking his emotions the whole time he'd been with her? Her vision blurred as tears forced their way to the surface, spilled over, and ran streaming down her cheeks.

"He cares for you," Billie shouted. "How could you do this to him?"

"How could Jenny do this to *him*?" Wayne retorted. "And what did he try to do to her? With *your* help?"

"I told him he had to tell Jenny the truth, but he wouldn't listen to me."

Wayne snorted. "You knew what he was doing. You could have told Jenny. You could have told *me*. But you didn't. No, instead, you helped your brother every step of the way. At least you and your brother are loyal to each other."

Billie winced as if she'd taken a physical blow, then she ran toward the waiting trucks, knocking over a watering can in the process.

Jenny gasped and sank to the ground. "Dear God, what have I done?"

"You haven't done anything," Wayne said, and placed his hand on her shoulder. "They were just using us."

Eight

THE FIREFIGHTERS, ALONG WITH TWO DOZEN able-bodied men, most of whom were ranchers, worked continuously for the next five days to stop the flames from spreading. Each day Wayne went with them, but the fire wasn't reported contained until the following weekend.

"Have you seen it?" Jenny asked, when Wayne returned.

"Not yet," he said, shaking his head. "The ranch is still off limits for another couple of hours."

A couple hours turned into a couple more, but at two o'clock in the afternoon the State Patrol allowed Wayne's truck through.

As they drove down the road toward Windy Meadows, Jenny stared in horror as the green rolling hills changed into landscape resembling barren wasteland. Charlie Pickett's ranch didn't have a single structure still standing. Her ranch would likely be in the same condition.

Jenny held her breath to stop the tears from spilling, but it only tightened the knot in her stomach.

She remembered her mother baking bread and canning jam in the kitchen and how the spicy aroma of apple pie could fill the entire house. She could still see her father sitting in the big easy chair in the living room next to the woodstove, reading the newspaper and smoking his pipe.

How many generations had slid down the old wooden banister next to the stairs? Or scrawled measurements of their children's growth in the hall closet? She'd hoped her own children's measurements would be there someday.

Perhaps she never had a chance to save the ranch, despite her best efforts. In any case, the scene over the next hill would tell all.

"Well, splint me together before I fall apart!" Harry exclaimed. "Jenny, are you seeing what I'm seeing?"

"The house is still standing."

"Saved by the finger of God, that's what it is," said Harry. "She's charred on all four sides but somehow still managed to make it through."

Jenny opened the door of the truck as soon as it pulled in the driveway and gasped. It was almost as if an enormous kettle of her uncle's black bean soup had been poured out over the whole land.

Parts of the charred ground, littered with a variety of melted debris, continued to steam. The hay barn was gone, along with the cow barns and the stable. The remains of the tractor shed lay in a pile of twisted metal.

What really sickened her, though, were the scorched carcasses of her entire herd of Black Angus cows. The animals had been out in the pasture, too close to the fire, and unable to escape the fast-spreading flames.

She cupped her hand over her mouth and nose. She'd never seen such a wretched sight. Or had to inhale such a ghastly smell. Bile rose in the back of her throat and she turned away.

Inside the house a different kind of horror awaited her. Although the structure was intact, the interior walls were blackened with soot. Cobwebs that before had hung in the corners unnoticed now eerily stood out in strands of black as if decorated for Halloween. The beds were covered in a fine film of gray ash and the scent of smoke was embedded in all of the furniture.

Every item in the house needed to be washed before any of them could move back in. *If* they were going to move back in. She, Harry, and Wayne had spent the last week at the Pine Hotel. Her financial deadline was only another week away and the rest of the scheduled pack trips had been canceled.

"I don't know what to do," Jenny confessed.

"You could ride." Harry handed her a newspaper and showed her a large ad.

She read aloud, "The annual Pine Tree Dash is to be held on July sixteenth at the East Creek Fairgrounds."

"You won the race three years ago," Harry reminded her, "and the prize money is twenty thousand dollars—enough to pay your bank debt."

"But Starfire hasn't raced in a long time,

and I don't have time to train another horse."

"You can't give up," Wayne said, coming to stand by Harry. "If you don't save the ranch, we'll all be a bunch of homeless beggars sleeping on the streets."

"There's not another horse that can jump better than that Thoroughbred in Okanogan County," said Harry.

"Not only do you need to be able to jump to win The Pine Tree Dash," Jenny said, gathering a rope to round up her horses from the hillside. "You need to be fast."

Could Starfire race again after all these years?

"I'll do it," Jenny said, making up her mind. "I'll sign Starfire up for the race—just as soon as I find him."

❖ ❖ ❖

JENNY WENT BACK OUTSIDE AND CALLED FOR HER horses. At first there was no response—then, in the distance, there were a couple of answering neighs. Twenty minutes later, Starfire walked slowly up the driveway—with a limp.

"Hey, big boy." She tried not to let disappointment get the best of her as she ran her hand over the swollen area above his hoof. "I guess you won't be racing."

❧   ❧   ❧

NICK FINISHED HELPING KEVIN WRAP THE FIRE hoses for the night and headed toward the Bets & Burgers Café. Irene Johnson had been nice enough to give him and Billie a place to stay. But for how long? Sooner or later, he'd have to face the fact he needed to book a flight back to New York.

He didn't want to leave Jenny behind. Somehow over the last few weeks the bet he'd made with her had become real. Only he didn't just want to marry her. He wanted her love. He wanted to hear the words.

Billie brought him a hamburger and sat beside him on the café steps. Dark rings circled her eyes, and she appeared thinner, more frail than he'd ever seen her.

"I'm so sorry, Nick. So sorry."

"I know."

They sat in silence, each in their own misery. Billie hadn't mentioned Wayne's name, but she didn't have to. Nick knew his sister had taken a secret liking to the blond ranch hand as much as he had come to care about Jenny. And now they'd lost them, along with any chance of paying off Billie's debt. Never had he felt so powerless.

How could he choose between Jenny and Billie?

Later, when he was alone, Nick sat on the edge of his borrowed bed mattress and dropped his head into his hands. He'd flown to Pine to deceive Jenny, and . . . he'd succeeded. He just hadn't realized how much his actions would cost him. He'd been so eager to make money to save his sister he'd become *obsessed*! Lost his values. Lost Jenny.

You don't deserve her. The accusing words tumbled about in his mind, and condemned him.

"God, help me," he pleaded aloud, and found himself on his knees without any conscious recollection of having slid down to them.

❖   ❖   ❖

JENNY OPENED THE CEDAR CHEST IN HER PARENTS' old bedroom and found her mother's wedding dress. The dress she'd hoped to wear someday.

"Does it smell like smoke?" Sarah asked.

Sarah Gardner, owner of the town bakery, had been her mother's best friend—until cancer separated them.

"No," she said, running a finger along the low-necked antique white gown with cap sleeves. She hugged it to her body, held out the long train with multiple inset lace designs, and looked at herself in the mirror. She was pathetic. Would she ever marry?

She kneeled next to the chest to search for her mother's jewelry and pulled out an old envelope.

"It's a letter from my great-great grandfather to my great-great grandmother."

She removed the fragile pages and read.

My dearest Katherine,

The new boys pan the river for gold with a zeal that disheartens my soul. Greed has taken hold of their hearts so they do not recognize true wealth. I told them I found more gold than they'd ever seen, indeed, a gold mine. I long for you to re-join me here in Pine so they can see firsthand the value

*of relationships. You are my most precious
treasure, my own pure gold, and your love
has made me a rich man.*

*Forever yours,
Shamus*

Sarah sighed. "Wow."

"*She* was the gold," Jenny said, and sat back
on her heels. "The gold mine he found was my
great-great grandmother."

"The men at the café will be disappointed,"
Sarah predicted. "They hoped the old journal
entry would lead to another gold rush."

"Me too." Jenny's shoulders slumped. "It
would have been nice to find a big gold nugget
in my yard. I could have saved the ranch. Now
I have nothing."

❧   ❧   ❧

THE HOT RAYS OF MIDDAY SUN STREAMED THROUGH
the bedroom window. Jenny pulled the sheet
higher to block the intrusive light. If only she
could block the memories.

She must be the stupidest girl on the planet
to have believed Nick cared for her. Heck, she'd

271

even daydreamed he was in *love* with her. And she with him.

Love.

A sharp ache cut through her stomach, and she rocked back and forth, gulping for air.

Was there no one out there in the world for her? Would she live the rest of her life alone?

She didn't like wallowing in self-pity any more than a knee-high pile of manure. Better to keep moving. Chores needed to be done—at least for one more day—and she didn't want to give Harry an excuse to start working again.

Jenny climbed out of bed, dressed in her barn clothes, and descended the stairs. She was halfway across the kitchen when the sound of shattering glass drew her attention. She changed direction and hurried into the living room.

"Wayne? Are you all right?"

His unshaven face hovered over the bar, the broken stem of a crystal goblet in his right hand and a bottle of scotch in his other.

"Sorry about the mess," Wayne said, his sullen expression instantly contrite.

"I'll clean up." Jenny bent to pick up the pieces and waved him off toward the door.

Wayne hesitated, and then sauntered away, taking the bottle of scotch with him.

Poor Wayne. Over the last few days she'd learned the ranch hand had a soft spot for Billie after all. How and when *that* had happened she didn't know, but it was clear Billie's absence had the same effect on him as Nick's absence had on *her*.

She stared at the broken glass stretched across the carpet, each shard a glistening reminder it had once been part of something beautiful.

❖   ❖   ❖

JENNY PULLED THE BLUE TARP OFF THE HAY BALES, loaded the wheelbarrow, and headed toward the makeshift corrals. The horses pawed the ground and snorted as she approached, anxious to get their food.

"Sorry I'm late," she said, and tossed them each a flake of alfalfa. "I know how impatient—"

Jenny did a double take. Starfire pranced with the others . . . without favoring the injured leg.

She slipped inside the pen and unwrapped

the bandage around the Thoroughbred's hock. No swelling. Could the horse be healed?

Jenny finished feeding the other horses. Then she rode Starfire bareback down to the river to see how much pressure he could handle. Starfire was restless. The horse pulled at the reins and wanted to fly. The rhythm of hooves increased the rhythm of Jenny's heart, and her thoughts headed straight toward the Pine Tree Dash.

The race started at four o'clock and the bank closed at five thirty. If she won, could she get the prize money to the manager in time? Her father once told her she was only a failure if she stopped trying—and, by golly, she wasn't going to give up now. Her ancestors were fighters, and so was she.

"C'mon, big boy," Jenny said, and turned Starfire back toward the ranch. "We have a race to win."

Nine

JENNY LOADED STARFIRE'S TACK INTO THE horse trailer, her mind bursting with renewed hope.

"Got company," Wayne warned.

She expected to see Sarah. Harry had said she'd planned to visit.

But it was that devil, Irene Johnson, who walked straight toward her. What the heck was *she* doing here?

In all the years Jenny had known her, Irene had never stepped foot on the ranch. Jenny turned from the trailer to face her. Both Harry and Wayne drew near.

"Hi, Jenny."

Jenny tried to think of something civil to say. Nothing came to mind.

Irene held up her hand. "Look. I know

what you think of me, but I thought you should know the truth."

Jenny crossed her arms over her chest. "What truth?"

"Billie owes a lot of money to an Atlantic City casino owner and Nick couldn't pull cash out of N.L.C. Industries to help her. The three parcels he owns in Pine were originally purchased to build a new shipping center. Nick thought he could sell them to get the money, but only one buyer was interested."

"Stewart Davenport," Jenny stated dryly.

"It was Davenport who put the idea in Nick's head to try to woo the land from you. He said he wouldn't buy Nick's land unless yours was included in the deal. Don't you see? Nick was just trying to get the money to protect his sister."

"It doesn't excuse what he did to *me*," Jenny said.

"Maybe Nick isn't asking for his behavior to be excused. Maybe all he hopes for is a little understanding and forgiveness," Irene said, and gave her a hard look before she walked away.

Jenny bit her lip, hating the way Irene made her feel. Like *she* was the bad guy.

❁ ❁ ❁

THE PINE TREE DASH DATED BACK TO 1906 AND WAS
open to both English and Western riders. There
were only two rules: stay on the trail, and no
endangering the horses or other competitors. It
wasn't a regulated event. Just a bunch of cowboys racing on a privately owned backcountry
trail. Each competitor paid an entry fee and the
first one across the finish line won the prize
money. This year they'd be using the Winding
River Trail that ran through Levi MacGowan's
property.

While Wayne, Sarah, and Harry went to
sign her in and get her number in the starting lineup, Jenny checked Starfire's leg. Still no
sign of weakness.

"Well, if it isn't the most popular bachelor-
ette in town," a voice purred close to her ear.
"Will you marry me, Jenny?"

She turned and stared at Travis Koenig—
her former fiancé. "What do you want?"

"I've come to wish you luck," he said.
"You'll need it if you plan to race against *me*."

"You entered the race?"

"Anything for the money, honey."

Jenny scowled. "You did me a favor when you didn't show up at the church."

"I did *myself* a favor," Travis said with a sneer. "I could never be tied to just one woman."

Jenny clenched her teeth as he walked away, and wished she'd never laid eyes on him.

❖ ❖ ❖

NICK SPRANG FROM THE TRUCK AND SCANNED THE maze of people, horses, and parked trailers to search for Jenny. He spotted her toward the far side of the field. She was lined up for the race atop Starfire. He'd never get to her in time if he tried to cut through the crowd. Instead, he circled along the wooded perimeter, but the starting whistle blew and the riders took off. He was too late.

"Chandler."

He recognized the voice behind him and froze. Slowly he turned around and there in front of him stood Vic Lucarelli—and six of his men.

❖ ❖ ❖

JENNY KEPT STARFIRE AT A CANTER AS THEY ROUNDED the first sharp corner of the trail. A fence bordered the right-hand side of the path and a burnt hedge bordered the left. They couldn't pass the riders in front of them. Then the hedge came to an end and the fifty-six riders entered in the race began to spread out. A space opened, Jenny took it, and urged Starfire forward.

A few minutes later they moved into the front half of the group, but her mind wandered back to Nick.

Where was he now? Was he thinking about her?

It's true, he hadn't been truthful with her about his identity. His intentions hadn't been honorable. But if he cared for her, didn't he deserve a second chance? If only she knew if he *did* care.

Amid the thunder of hooves, the sharp crack of a whip rang in her ears and Travis Koenig drove his Palomino straight in front of her. Starfire veered. If she hadn't kept a firm grip on the reins, the Thoroughbred could have slipped off the steep embankment.

She readjusted her seat, and would have called Travis several of the names she'd heard Billie use, except Travis was already too far ahead to hear.

"Go after him, Jenny." Kevin Forester rode Blue Devil up on her left. "You can do it. Take the bull by the horns."

Easy to say, harder to do.

As the elevation increased, so did the amount of sharp turns up the craggy hillside. The switchbacks made it difficult once again for anyone to pass, and to her dismay, Travis remained more than six riders ahead.

A rumble sounded above and she glanced at the cliff on her left in horror.

"Rockslide," someone shouted.

Jenny's adrenaline shot into high gear as she and Starfire raced to avoid the onslaught of stones tumbling down the mountain. The ground was loose from the forest fire. Without the trees and bushes to hold the rocks in place, the slightest disturbance could initiate a slide. For one fateful second she cringed and thought they'd roll to their death. Then the roar of the avalanche fell away from her and echoed across the valley below.

"That was close," Kevin yelled from behind.

It was indeed. She looked back over her shoulder and drew in a sharp breath.

Four feet of debris blocked the path and

brought the race to a premature end for half the riders entered.

To win, she needed to reach the band of riders in front of her who vied for first place.

The trail widened and the trees parted to reveal an open field. Jenny loosened the reins and leaned forward in the saddle. Starfire gave a shrill whinny and picked up his pace from a canter to a full run.

They passed three riders, a fourth, a fifth. Travis Koenig, riding the Palomino, was fifty yards ahead.

Nick, too, had always been one step ahead. He'd challenged her, drawn her out of her self-imposed hermit status, and reintroduced her to the world again.

What if she lost the race? Lost the ranch? Where would she go? What would she do? Her thoughts swirled so fast she couldn't think straight. Good thing her horse knew what to do.

Starfire jumped over a fallen log, raced around the fire-damaged bridge, and splashed straight through a shallow network of streams. They passed more riders whose mounts had begun to tire. She lost sight of Travis when they rounded the curve, but he had to be close.

She'd been on this trail dozens of times with Levi and her father when they hunted elk. A half mile remained and she couldn't waste a single second. Every moment, every step, from this point on, mattered.

And yet, she continued to think of Nick, his silver-gray eyes upon her, his expression earnest, as he asked her to trust him. It wasn't like her to not let someone explain, but she had been too upset at the time to hear him out. Now she wondered what he might have had to say.

Starfire was exhausted. She could feel the tension in his muscles. He wouldn't be able to last much longer.

"C'mon, boy," she whispered. "You can do it."

The noise of the horse's hooves drummed in Jenny's ears as they drew up behind the Palomino. A fallen tree crossed the path ahead. Two and a half feet high. No problem for her to jump. Starfire rode English.

What would Travis do? His western saddle horn would gouge his stomach if he jumped, but it *could* be done.

The Palomino tried to pull the reins out of Travis's hands, but the former rodeo star held on and refused to relinquish control. He smacked his crop against the horse's hindquarters and headed straight toward the log.

Drat! Travis was going to jump, despite the consequences. Circling the tree would waste too much time. If she were in his place, she'd attempt the jump, too.

Jenny held her breath, dread already rushing into the pit of her stomach as the Palomino's muscles flexed. If the Palomino made it over, Travis would win.

Then the Palomino pulled up short at the last second. Pitched Travis sideways. Starfire's muscles bunched and a second later she and Starfire soared into the sky. Sun kissed the top of her head. Wind blew back her hair. They rose higher and higher as if lifted by a giant hand. Jenny laughed. Giddy. She was *free*.

The horses, the house, the fields, everything she loved that hung in the balance of this jump . . . would finally be free of outside threat.

Loud cheers and spontaneous applause greeted them as Starfire's hooves met the ground and they crossed the finish line.

They did it. They won.

Jenny broke into a smile, and wrapped her arms around her beloved horse.

"That's my good boy," she whispered.

Starfire's ears twitched at the sound of her voice, and he whinnied his acceptance of the praise.

She'd never know why the Palomino refused the jump. Maybe the horse didn't have much experience. Or maybe it just didn't like Travis.

Harry came over and chuckled, gave the Thoroughbred an affectionate pat. "See? Old age doesn't mean you're out of the race. I think we both have a bit more life in us."

Kevin, Charlie, David, and several others also came to offer their congratulations.

"I knew you could do it, girl." Levi's old wrinkled face beamed as he handed her the official prize check.

"The bank closes in fifteen minutes," said Harry. He took Starfire's reins. "You have to hurry."

Jenny glanced from her truck at the far end of the parking lot to David Wilson's, about fifteen feet away.

"David, can you give me a ride?"

The rancher whipped his keys out of his pocket. "You bet I can."

284

Ten

DAVID WILSON SHOULD HAVE BEEN ARRESTED for the way he sped into town. The truck shot around turns, spit gravel, and squealed louder than a wayward missile.

Jenny braced one hand on the dashboard while the other gripped the edge of her seat. She didn't know whether to be scared or thankful, but her need to get to the bank had her leaning toward thankful.

The clock above the building read 5:20. Jenny looked through the large bay window as David squealed to a stop, and saw the financial manager still at his desk. She and David hopped out of the front of the truck, while Wayne, Kevin, and Levi, who hadn't wanted to be left behind, climbed out of the back.

Jenny hurried to the bank entrance.

"Jenny, wait!"

She hesitated. Turned around. "Billie?"

Nick's sister ran toward her. *"They're going to kill him!* I don't know what to do. If I go over to them they'll kill *me!*"

Wayne put a hand on Billie's shoulder. "No one is going to harm you."

"I owe Lucarelli a hundred grand. He insists on getting part of the money today. It's all my fault. Everything that's happened is all my fault. I never should have gambled, never should have cheated. Now the guy I owe is *here* with six men and they have Nick . . ."

"I won't let him stand alone," Wayne said, his voice firm. "Where are they?"

"Behind the Bets & Burgers Café."

Jenny glanced down at the check in her hand, more money than she'd ever held in her entire life. She could either save the ranch from foreclosure . . . or she could save Nick by paying part of Billie's debt.

She turned away from the bank and hurried after Wayne and Billie.

When she rounded the corner of the café she saw them. Seven men, dressed in various shades of black and blue, one of them grasping the front of Nick's shirt.

"*Stop!*" she shouted. "I have the money Billie owes you."

The men all looked at her with surprise, including Nick, as she stepped forward and placed the prize check into the nearest man's hands.

The man smiled. "Thank you, but the debt has already been paid."

"It has?" Jenny gasped as he handed her check back to her. "How?"

She didn't wait for an answer. She ran as fast as she could, back to the bank, but it was too late. The bank had closed. And she missed her deadline.

Jenny stood there, in front of the door for several long minutes, looking at her reflection in the glass.

She didn't know where she would live now, but as long as she was with Nick, she'd be okay. Because she loved him and love wasn't tied to a place. It resided in the heart. Stewart Davenport could take her ranch away, but she'd keep the love of her family safe in her heart forever.

Crossing the street, she stepped through the café's open door. The room was packed. Tales spread within seconds in a small town, and Jenny figured the people couldn't wait to see Nick any more than she could.

Where *was* Nick?

The broad shoulders of two big burly men blocked her view of the back counter, but her heart skipped a beat at the sound of his voice.

"I'm flying back to New York tonight," Nick said to the crowd.

"What about Jenny?" Levi called out. "You still have a few minutes left to win the bet."

Jenny dug her toes into the tips of her boots, listening, but still unable to see.

"No," he said, his voice strained. "I blew it. Jenny will never marry me now."

Never marry him? *No!* Her heart hammered as she squeezed past the two big men and stepped into the open space before them.

"Twenty thousand dollars says she will."

Jenny waved the check she received for the race and the crowd hushed.

She didn't look at them. Her attention was fixed solely on Nick, whose gaze locked on to hers the moment she spoke.

"You want to marry me?"

"Yes."

Nick's expression remained guarded. She

couldn't tell what he was thinking. Did he really care for her or had the light in his eyes, the passion in his kisses all been an act? Her stomach clenched as she waited for a sign.

"Jenny," Nick said, his voice slow and even, "I traded Charlie Pickett my three land parcels for his early fire-insurance money. I used it to pay off both your ranch and Billie's debt this afternoon."

"You mean the ranch is still mine?"

"Forever and ever."

Jenny gasped. "And you?"

The taut muscles in Nick's face relaxed, his eyes sparkled . . . And the wide smile he gave her dispelled every fear that had hovered at the edge of her heart.

Jenny wasn't sure who moved first, but a moment later she was wrapped in a fierce hug, and she was laughing and crying at the same time. Warmth flooded over her and she became light-headed, as if she'd sipped too much of Levi MacGowan's home-brewed whiskey.

"Why?" Nick asked. "Why did you try to trade the money to save Windy Meadows for me?"

Jenny pressed her cheek against his chest,

the truth never more clear. "I could never love a place as much as I love you."

Nick pulled back with a start. "What did you say?"

"I love you," she repeated, her whole heart behind each word.

Nick grinned. "Will you marry me right now?"

"Yes."

"Don't do it, Jenny!" Charlie shouted. "It's almost six o'clock. If you wait eight more minutes, you'll win the bet."

Jenny shook her head. "I don't want to wait another second."

Nick looked at the man behind him. "Reverend Thornberry, did you hear that?"

The minister furrowed his brows. "I'm afraid I did."

Nick took her hand and gazed down at her with more passion than she'd ever believed possible.

"I love you, too, Jenny."

Reverend Thornberry began to recite the traditional passages. Then he rolled his eyes heavenward and threw up his hands. "May

God help you, I now pronounce you husband and wife."

Nick drew her close and kissed her, his lips warm and tender, and full of promises for the future.

"Fifty dollars says their first kid is a boy," Levi called out.

Cheers soared into the air, and empty drink glasses smashed wildly around them, as more and more wagers began to be placed.

Nick smiled against her lips and Jenny couldn't help but laugh. She was more than willing to be part of *this* bet!

The World of

DEBBIE MACOMBER

When you wish upon a star, do you ever think it will come true? Maybe not on any ordinary day, but Christmastime is when it's most possible—especially if you have a trio of charismatic angels fighting for love on your side! These stories will warm your heart, feed your faith, and show you that miracles can happen. Curl up on the couch, find a sparkly star, and discover how love found a way through the troubles, the heartbreak, and the doubt.

A Season of Angels

Shirley, Goodness, and Mercy—a pack of earnest, yet zany angels—are on a mission to fulfill their Christmas task: answering the prayers of three weary mortals. There's nine-year-old Timmy Potter, who wants a father, even though his mother has given up on men. Monica Fischer, after searching high and low, just wants to find a husband and a home of her own. And Leah Lundberg, a maternity nurse, would like a baby to complete her family. Answering prayers is easy for these angels, but there's a catch this time: each granter must teach their grantee a lesson before their desires can be fulfilled . . .

$\mathcal{M}$ONICA'S THE TALL ONE ON THE TOP RISER," Gabriel said, pointing out the earthling to Goodness. Like Mercy, Gabriel held a special fondness for this prayer ambassador, who, again like Mercy, possessed certain character traits that left him with misgivings. If it weren't for the business of the Christmas season, he wouldn't have assigned Goodness such a difficult case.

Unfortunately he had little choice and of those ambassadors left, Goodness was his best chance of seeing this prayer to fruition. If only he could guarantee that Goodness would stay away from television and movie screens. The incident of her showing up on an in-flight movie and using John Wayne's voice to warn everyone of approaching turbulence continued to rankle. He'd counseled her on a number of occasions, but to no avail.

"I know what you're thinking," Goodness said, looking up at him with eyes filled with innocent promise. "I won't pull any more stunts with humans. I've learned my lesson."

"You're sure this time?"

Goodness glanced toward Monica and nodded eagerly.

Gabriel wished he shared her confidence. His own gaze drifted toward Monica Fischer. Her name was a familiar one as her father, a man after God's own heart, often included her in his prayers. Monica came from a strong religious background. With her father serving as the pastor, Monica had been raised in the church. It was ironic that what the young woman lacked was faith when she was surrounded on all sides by it. Instead Monica was deeply religious and had yet to distinguish the differences between faith and religion.

"She's lovely," Goodness claimed, locking her wings together. "Finding Monica a husband won't be the least bit difficult, not when she's so outwardly beautiful. God must have a special man in mind for her."

"He does," Gabriel agreed with some reluctance, wondering just how much he should explain to this inexperienced ambassador. Goodness would learn everything she needed to know soon enough, he decided. The information he had would overwhelm her now. Soon enough Goodness would recognize exactly what God had planned for Monica Fischer.

The angel focused her attention on him, her eyes wide and questioning, awaiting an explanation. "What is it I must teach her?"

Gabriel drew in a deep breath and explained. "I fear Monica's steeped in the juices of her own self-righteousness. She struggles to be good under her own power and ignores all the help made available to her through faith."

Goodness sighed with heartfelt sympathy. "She must be miserable."

"No," Gabriel returned without hesitation, "she just makes everyone else feel that way. Monica's complicated her life with a long list of rights and wrongs and dos and don'ts. Her head's so clouded with matters unrelated to faith that she's lost sight of what it means to be a child of God. Her struggles are useless when everything has already been done for her. All she need do is ask." But Gabriel wasn't telling Goodness anything new. The earth was populated with those who looked for redemption through religion.

"The poor dear."

Gabriel didn't view Monica in those terms. It was her type that caused him the greatest concern. While Monica struggled to lead people to God, her sanctimonious ways often steered them in the opposite direction.

"She sings very well," Goodness commented.

Gabriel nodded. "She's gifted in several areas."

"I shouldn't have any trouble teaching what she needs to know before Christmas."

How confident Goodness sounded, Gabriel noticed. He sighed inwardly, wondering once more how much he should explain, then decided it would be best not to discourage Goodness's enthusiasm. She'd discover everything she needed to know soon enough.

"The man God has for her is ready for a wife?"

Gabriel was beginning to feel a twinge of guilt. "Yes, and eager. Very eager. Only he doesn't know it yet, but you won't have to worry about him. Monica's the one who needs you."

"Then I'll do everything within my power to help her."

"You're ready?" Gabriel asked, thinking he'd best send her soon before he said too much. This request would be a learning experience for this young prayer ambassador as well as for her charge. All he could do was hope for the best.

"Let's go," Goodness said, impatient to leave the splendor of heaven and walk incognito into a dull, sin-cloaked world.

Gabriel watched as Goodness floated down from heaven, thinking humans were right about one thing. God often did work in mysterious ways and never more so than in this instance. Gabriel was confident of one thing. Neither Goodness nor Monica Fischer would ever be the same again.

The Trouble with Angels

Heaven's famous celestial trio are back again! When angels Shirley, Goodness, and Mercy receive three last-ditch Christmas prayers from some very lonely souls in Los Angeles, they're ready to help. Irrepressible and quirky, the angels are ready to serve up a hearty helping of faith, mend a few broken hearts, and bring hope to those in despair. Unfortunately, it will take more than usual to repair these forsaken few. But there's no wish these angels can't grant, and as headstrong and unstoppable as they are, they're faithful that they'll be able to deliver the best holiday gift of all: love!

*T*HAT'S CATHERINE," CABRIEL SAID, STARING down upon the earthly scene below.

Mercy was intrigued. The archangel had claimed she'd like Catherine, and Mercy had, immediately. "What a dear, sweet woman she is."

Gabriel nodded. "Catherine Goodwin has a heart after God's own."

"What about Blythe Holmes?" Mercy was anxious to learn what she could about the younger woman. "Is she the right wife for Ted?"

Gabriel folded his massive wings against his back. "I don't have the answer to that. But I'm sure within a short amount of time you'll discover that for yourself."

"You know who *I* think he should marry."

"Who?" Gabriel's head bent back with surprise.

"Well, we just met her for a moment or two, but I think Joy Palmer—"

"Joy Palmer?" Gabriel said loudly enough to ruffle Mercy's delicate feathers. Sometimes the archangel forgot how much larger he was than a mere prayer ambassador.

"I realize we only just met her, but didn't you notice how gentle and caring she is toward Catherine and the other residents at Wilshire Grove?"

Gabriel studied Mercy for a lengthy, uncomfortable moment. "Yes, but that doesn't mean she'd make Ted Griffin a good wife."

"Catherine likes her," Mercy felt obliged to remind him.

"She's also fond of Emily, Thelma, Lucille, and the other ladies on the library committee, but I don't see you matchmaking Ted with any of them."

"That would be ridiculous," Mercy said, not understanding Gabriel's lack of insight. All this should have been obvious to him. "Those women aren't anywhere close to Ted's age. Joy Palmer is a mere five years younger."

Gabriel crossed his arms as if to say he'd like nothing better than to end their conversation.

"Futhermore, I saw the look that came into Joy's eyes when Ted first arrived. It's clear to me that you're simply not that well versed in the area of human romance."

"And you are?"

"I know a little about romance," Mercy admitted. "Enough to know *interested* when I see it, and Joy was definitely interested."

"I won't have you pulling any of your funny business. Understand?"

Mercy put on her most injured look. "I wouldn't dream of doing a—"

"Yes, you would," Gabriel interrupted testily. "I'm telling you right now, I won't put up with any of it."

"Haven't I given you my word of honor?"

"A lot of good that did me last year," Gabriel mumbled under his breath. Then, with little fanfare, he lifted his massive arms, parting the thick clouds, and ushered them back into the prayer room.

Both Shirley and Goodness were waiting for her.

"Well?" Goodness asked.

"Gabriel was right," Mercy said, almost breathless, she was so eager to tell her friends everything she'd found out about Catherine

Goodwin. She could handle this prayer request with one wing tied behind her back! "I'm really pleased to work with such a wonderful older woman."

"Just wait until I tell you what I learned," Shirley said, slumping onto a chair and raising her feet onto the ottoman. Both her arms dangled over the sides as if it demanded too much energy to life them. "I'm afraid I'm going to need help. Lots and lots of help."

"You've got it," Goodness assured her. "Really, Shirley, this is the beauty of the three of us working together."

"We're a team."

"A team," Gabriel repeated as if the idea of the three of them assigned to the same city should have been outlawed.

"Lighten up, Gabe," Goodness said, and pressed her hands agains her hip. "We're going to be so good you won't even know we're on assignment."

"Lost Angeles could use a bit of our help," Mercy said, thinking about all she'd seen in those brief moments allotted her.

"I don't think California's prepared for the likes of you three," Gabriel grumbled.

"None of these prayer requests should take long," Mercy said, feeling confident. As far as she could see, all she had to do was subtly steer Ted Griffin's interest toward a certain service director and leave the rest up to the two of them. She'd do it, Mercy vowed, without causing Gabriel any grief, either. She was, after all, an angel of her word.

"I need all three of you back here soon," Gabriel reminded them.

"How soon?" This came from Shirley.

Mercy didn't know the full extent of her friend's assignment, but the case seemed to be troubling Shirley. Whe she'd finished with hers, which shouldn't take any more than two or three days, she'd give her friend a hand.

"Before Christmas," Gabrield told them sternly.

"Before Christmas?" Goodness repeated. "But that's impossible."

"Nothing is impossible with God," the archangel reminded them.

Shirley released a long sigh. "I wonder how long it's been since he visted L.A."

Touched by Angels

In a city with buildings that touch the clouds, the sky is the limit! And luckily for three hardened New Yorkers, our favorite angels are here to prove it. Shirley, Goodness, and Mercy are back again to bestow divine inspiration and hope where it's needed most. Winging in from Heaven, these angels will grant more than just a Christmas prayer—they'll leave these deserving souls with a gift that will last them a lifetime: the gift of love.

BRYNN'S WHISPERED PRAYER FLUTTERED PAST the chipped blackboard, echoed silently through the scarred halls, as it winged its way toward heaven. The request soared, swiftly spanning the distance between man and God. Carried on the brisk winds of faith, guided by devotion, navigated by love, it arrived fresh and bright at the very feet of the Archangel Gabriel.

"Brynn Cassidy," Gabriel repeated slowly as he flipped through the cumbersome book, marking the entry. He was writing when he glanced up to find Shirley, Goodness, and Mercy standing directly across the desk from him. He'd never seen the three look more—he hated the term—angelic. Their wings were neatly folded in place and they smiled serenely as if the world were at their feet.

"It's that time of year again," Goodness reminded him, grinning broadly.

Gabriel's hand tightened around the quill pen. Heaven help him, he was going to be left to deal with these three lovable troublemakers once more.

"Time of year for what?" he asked. Gabriel was playing dumb in a stalling effort. For the past two years this trio of prayer ambassadors had visited earth, working their own unique brand of miracles. A sort of divine intervention run amuck.

"We'd like to try our hand in the Big Apple," Mercy explained with limited patience. It was apparent she was eager to get her assignment and be on her way. "We've been looking forward to working together again," she reminded him primly. "One would assume that with the success of the past two years we'd have proven ourselves beyond question."

"We don't mean to be impertinent," Goodness inserted, glaring at her fellow prayer ambassador, "but I find myself agreeing with Mercy."

"Brynn Cassidy," Shirley repeated softly, reading over Gabriel's shoulder.

Gabriel deliberately closed the huge book, cutting off Shirley's view. The last thing he needed was for the former guardian angel to take a hankering for this particular assignment.

The students of Manhattan High would require a far more experienced angel than Shirley. Why, her tender heart would be mush by the end of a week, working with this group of adolescents. Frankly, Gabriel didn't expect Brynn Cassidy to last long herself.

Gabriel knew all about the young teacher. Her mother and grandfather had been praying for her for several years. As far as Gabriel was concerned, Brynn Cassidy was far more suited to teaching the proper young ladies of St. Mary Academy. Manhattan High was a graveyard of lost souls. An unseen storm cloud had settled over the school, feeding on tears yet to be shed and broken promises. Brynn's humble faith was like a newborn lamb placed in the midst of ravenous wolves. She'd quickly be devoured. Naturally Gabriel would do what he could to aid her, but one ill-equipped prayer ambassador would hardly be sufficient.

"Brynn needs me," Shirley said, looking him squarely in the eye.

"She needs an army. I don't mean to discourage you," Gabriel said, feeling mildly guilty, "I'm sure we'll find a more appropriate assignment for you. A less complicated request," he muttered more to himself than to Shirley.

As he recalled, a prayer request had come in that morning from a teenage girl in Boston who needed a date for prom night. Surely Shirley could scrounge up a decent young man. As for Goodness and Mercy, why, there were any number of less demanding requests with which to occupy them.

"Give me a minute," he said, flipping through the unwieldy book, finding a page, and running his index finger down the large number of entries. "I'm sure I'll come up with something appropriate for each of you."

"No arguments?" Goodness asked, her eyes wide with surprise.

"Wow, maybe we have proven ourselves."

"I want to talk to Goodness about Hannah Morganstern," Gabriel said, his brow creased with contemplation.

"Yes," Goodness answered excitedly.

"Her family owns one of the most popular delis in all of New York," the Archangel went on to explain.

Goodness and Mercy looked at each other

and squealed with delight. The two joined hands and danced a happy jig around his desk, kicking up their heels.

"What about me?" Mercy asked, breathless with excitement.

"Jenny Lancaster," Gabriel said decisively. "She moved to New York from Custer, Montana, three years ago, hoping to make a name for herself on Broadway."

"Has she?"

"No," Gabriel said with a sigh of regret. "It's time to go home, only she can't bear to face that. You see, she doesn't want to disappoint her family, and I'm afraid she's stretched the truth and told them things that weren't altogether true. You're going to have to help her make the decision."

"I can do it."

"Without moving the Statue of Liberty?" Gabriel demanded.

"That's kid stuff," Goodness muttered.

"Maybe so, but is Rockefeller Center safe?"

The two found little humor in his question. It was then that Gabriel noticed that Shirley had disappeared.

"Where's Shirley?"

Goodness and Mercy glanced over their shoulders. "I haven't a clue."

"I didn't see her leave."

Gabriel had a sneaking suspicion he already knew where the prayer ambassador had disappeared to. "Wait here," he instructed impatiently. He raised his massive arms and with one wide, sweeping motion parted the clouds of heaven and descended from paradise to the mundane world.

He found Shirley right where he suspected: in an inner-city classroom, keeping a close watch on a young, inexperienced schoolteacher.

Mrs. Miracle

It's Christmastime, but widower Seth Webster is feeling anything but jolly. With two rambunctious twin boys to look after by himself, and a mess of a house that leaves every capable nanny running in the opposite direction, this single dad needs a miracle. So when Mrs. Merkle arrives, she proves to be the answer to Seth's prayers. This warm, wise, and very patient nanny—who the kids have appropriately nicknamed "Mrs. Miracle"—has spread a contagious epidemic of laughter, sass, and courage. She's even convinced Seth to approach Reba, a beautiful travel agent who's had her heart broken. With a little Christmas cheer, some Merkle magic, and a whole lot of faith, Seth and Reba might find their own miracle: a second chance at love.

I CAN'T TELL YOU HOW SORRY I AM." SETH SIN-
cerely hoped he sounded regretful, but
he doubted he'd be any more successful in pulling the wool over this woman's eyes than he
was with his own children.

"I'm afraid I don't share your regrets. Of all
the positions I've held in my fifteen-year history of domestic service, I can never remember
having to deal with a worse pair of undisci-
plined children. I understood when I accepted
the position that the twins were considered a
handful, but this is ridiculous."

"They're only six."

"Exactly. Six going on thirteen. I don't have
a moment's peace from dawn to dusk. Those
two are constantly underfoot. They're savages,
I tell you. Savages."

"I've already explained to the kids that
goldfish can't live in Jell-O," Seth said. "I realize it was a shock to open the refrigerator and
find the goldfish bowl filled with lemon Jell-O
and three small fish."

"The problem with the goldfish was the tip of the iceberg," she responded, and grimaced.

"Okay, okay, so maybe those water bazookas weren't such a good idea. I didn't think they'd turn them on you." By sheer willpower, Seth managed to squelch a smile. One gloriously sunny autumn afternoon, he had been washing the car while the twins raced across kingdom come, soaking each other with their fancy water guns. When Mrs. Hampston stepped onto the porch Judd and Jason had guilelessly turned their weapons on her. To put it mildly, the housekeeper had not been amused. To Seth's way of thinking, a little water never hurt anyone.

"It isn't the Jell-O incident or the water bazookas. It isn't even having to routinely dig little green army men out of the bathtub drain. It's you."

"Me?" Seth demanded defensively. He'd bent over backward to keep the peace with Mrs. Hampston, and now she was accusing him!

"You know absolutely nothing about being a father."

Seth's mouth snapped shut. Like all good

military strategists, she attacked his weakest point. He had no argument.

"The twins are your children, Mr. Webster, not your friends, and not cute pets. They need a firm, guiding hand. As far as I can see, you're no example for them. None whatsoever. Swearing is one thing, but to put it bluntly, you're a slob."

Seth knew she was right. He was an absentminded professor, his head filled with work, the kids, and everything else. He didn't mean to be untidy, it just happened that way. He constantly lost and found himself. Mundane things like remembering to fill up the car with gas escaped him. The other morning, to her disgust, Mrs. Hampston had found his shoes in the refrigerator. Seth vaguely recalled putting them there.

"If you'd be willing to give me another chance . . ."

"I've already assured you I won't."

"Yes, but finding another housekeeper might prove difficult just now."

"I'm sure it will be, but that isn't my problem."

Seth leaned against the door, wondering

where to turn to next. Mrs. Hampston had been his last hope. The agency didn't have anyone else to send. He didn't know what he would do, where he would turn.

"Frankly, Mr. Webster," the woman stated smugly, "it isn't a housekeeper you need, it's a miracle."

They say love comes when you're not looking for it. For the heroes and heroines of these romances, that couldn't be more true! It's an explosive firework that sparks an unexpected romance in the hearts of these characters.

Trusting in the intangibles that come with caring about someone proves to be all it takes to make happy endings possible.

Morning Comes Softly

When you've been alone for as long as timid Louisiana librarian Mary Warner, you start to wonder if you'll ever find love. Tragedy-stricken Travis Thompson, a Montana rancher, is muddling through those same worries as he cares for three orphaned children who desperately need a mother. Advertising for a wife in a personals ad feels crazy, until Travis hears from Mary, daring to take a chance on an unseen man. Both nervous to embark on their new life together, they find that, with a little warmth and trust, miracles can go a long way—and love can last even longer.

Dear Mr. Travis Thompson:

I am writing in response to your advertisement in the Billings Gazette. My name is Mary Warner. I'm thirty-two and have never been married. I'm currently employed as head librarian in Petite, Louisiana.

In regard to your ad, I meet the requirements you stated. I'm an excellent cook, my specialty being boneless chicken with oyster dressing and gingersnap gravy. My sweet fig pie recipe won a blue ribbon two years back, and I'd be more than pleased to share the recipe with your family, if you so desire. I also serve up a respectable etouffee and apple pie.

As for my ability to sew, I am an accomplished seamstress and have been making my own clothes from the age of sixteen. Over the years I've sewn several complicated patterns for friends and family, including my best friend's wedding dress, which entailed five hundred pearls to be stitched on by hand.

Now, in regard to my ability to sing. I have been a first soprano for the Petite Regular Baptist Church for the past ten years and have given several solo performances. I've sung at weddings, funerals, birthday parties, and anniversaries. If you wish to review a tape of my singing voice, I will willingly supply you with one.

Other than the talents you requested, I'll add that I come from hardy southern stock with roots that can be traced back as far as the early 1600s. Some of my relatives include a Spanish conquistador, a soldier who fought in the bayous with Jackson, and an Acadian exile. There's no doubt in my mind that the blood of more than one pirate has mingled with the Warner line.

Having lived in Petite all my life, I'm afraid I know next to nothing about cattle and the like. Nor have I ever lived on a ranch. I do suffer from a few minor allergies, but to the best of my knowledge hay isn't one of them.

If you would be willing to consider me as a candidate for your wife, then you may write to me at the address listed on the top of the page.

Respectfully,
Mary S. Warner

Mary mailed the letter first thing the following morning, before she could entertain second thoughts. They came anyway, almost immediately after she'd dropped the letter in the mail slot, followed by an entire day in which she chastised herself for yielding to the fantasy.

She was too old. Too quiet. Her roots were in the South, her heritage, everything that was important to her. Travis Thompson and those three children wouldn't want her. He'd want a wife who was young and pretty. Not someone whose most appealing feature was blue eyes.

Only . . . only she could cook and sew and sing. And that was all Travis Thompson had claimed he wanted. He hadn't said a word about requiring a beauty queen and a fashion model.

The response came back so fast that it made her head spin. Within a week she was clenching an envelope postmarked Grandview, Montana.

Dear Miss Warner,

Thank you for your kind letter, which the children and I have read with interest. Since you've been so forthright about yourself, I figured it's only fair to share a bit of my own background. I'm a cattle rancher, age 36. Like you, I've never been married.

My brother Lee and I were born and raised in Grandview. Lee married Janice a few years out of high school, but the two of them were killed several months back in an auto accident. I was granted custody of Jim, Scotty, and Beth Ann. They're the only reason I need a wife.

If you're looking for romance, fancy words, and expensive gifts, then I'll tell you right now, I haven't got the money or the inclination for such things. My brother and his wife are gone, and I've got my hands full dealing with their youngsters. I don't have time to properly court a woman. I need a wife and these children need a mother.

My spread has over 15,000 acres, and I make a decent wage when the beef prices are fair, but I'm not a wealthy man, so if that's what you're thinking, then I suggest you withdraw your name from consideration.

I'm honest, although there are some who would question that. I work hard and play just as hard. I drink a little now and again, but I don't chew or smoke. I enjoy a game of poker with the men, but rarely play more than once or twice a month. I kinda hate to give that up. I swear a little, but Beth Ann's taken it upon herself to clean up my language. I'm not much of a talker and keep mostly to myself.

Each of the children have a question. Jim thanks you for the offer of the recipe for your sweet fig pie but wants to know if you can bake chocolate-chip cookies. He figures if you can cook up gingersnap gravy, you'll probably know how to cook just about anything.

Scotty says he doesn't care if you can sew wedding dresses. He's more anxious to find out if you can mend the tear in his favorite plaid shirt. He won't let me try since I ruined Beth Ann's church dress trying to fix the ruffle.

Beth Ann's biggest concern is if you can make up songs and would be willing to sing them to her when she goes to bed the way her mother used to do.

As you might have guessed, I sincerely lack any domestic talents. I can't carry a tune any better than I can cook.

If you decide after reading this that you're

still interested, then please write again. A picture would be appreciated.

Sincerely,
Travis J. Thompson

Mary read Travis's letter straight through, twice. She read it so many times in the next few hours that the top edges of the pages started to curl. Of course she'd hoped to hear from him, but she hadn't allowed herself the luxury of believing he would actually respond to her letter. A thousand times she regretted the wording. She should have said this, deleted that. For days she'd been tormenting herself, regretting whatever weakness had possessed her to answer the Billings ad.

The instant she heard from Travis, all her doubt evaporated. She was thrilled.

One Night

For KUTE radio's spunky, funny DJ Carrie Johnson, adoration from her fans and co-workers come easy . . . except for that stuffy newscaster, Kyle Harris, whose disapproval is crystal clear. So when their feuding tension becomes too much for the workplace, their boss orders them to fire up a friendship, or *be* fired. Stuck together on a days-long road trip, they need to learn to get along fast, before they kill each other. But what started as a tentative truce soon leads to attraction—and what began as a quest to save their jobs might bring them something much more rewarding.

*F*ROM THE FIRST DAY, CARRIE FELT KYLE'S mild contempt. It might have been her imagination, but she doubted it. He thought of her as silly and artificial, and she viewed him as a curmudgeon. The fact that he shared the same political views as her father hadn't endeared him to her either.

"Is this all because of Kyle's beard?"

A shadow of a smile quivered at the edges of Clyde's mouth, but he suppressed it. "In part," he said. No amusement leaked into his voice.

"It was all in fun."

Carrie wanted to shake herself for the things she'd said. She hadn't meant to insult Kyle by suggesting he had a face made for radio. It was a joke. She should have known better.

"The ratings for my show doubled that week," she reminded him.

"Are you suggesting we give you an award?" Clyde's voice rose half an octave in irritation.

"He hasn't grown it back," Carrie said, wanting to make light of the event. She found Kyle's clean-shaven face to be surprisingly appealing. Her perception of him had changed. Without the beard, his jaw was lean and strongly defined, giving him a distinctly rugged appeal she would never have guessed was there. She hated to admit how curious she'd been to discover the man behind the mask.

Clyde couldn't seem to decide if he wanted to stand or sit. He got out of his chair as if he were suddenly uncomfortable, walked over to the window that overlooked downtown Kansas City, and gripped his hands behind his back.

"Have my ratings gone down?" she asked nervously.

"No," Clyde admitted. "Don't misunderstand me, Carrie, you've done a good job. That's not the problem. The reason I'm terminating you is because of what's going on between you and Kyle. The rest of us aren't blind. We all work together, and we can't be one big happy family with the two of you constantly at each other's throat."

"I'm not the only one to blame," she said, to defend herself. It wasn't as if she'd started a one-woman war against Kyle Harris. He'd tossed out his own fair share of innuendoes and insults.

"It's become an issue with the staff," Clyde said. "In the beginning it was like a game; everyone got a kick out of the way you taunted each other. It isn't amusing anymore. What started out as fun has become destructive to the entire station."

She had no defense. "But—"

"I don't have any choice," Clyde said, cutting her off. He shifted his feet as if struggling to find a comfortable stance. "I did what was necessary. I canned you both."

"You fired *both* of us?" Carrie bolted out of the chair before she could stop herself.

"Don't misunderstand me," Clyde said, fixing his steady gaze on her. "This isn't something I wanted to do, but it'd be impossible to keep one of you and let the other go. Not unless I wanted a mutiny."

Carrie appreciated his predicament; she just didn't happen to like it. "But you're willing to reconsider if Kyle and I can reach some sort of agreement?" she asked, sinking back into the hard wooden chair. It would be easier to negotiate peace talks in the Middle East, but she'd try anything in order to keep her position at the station. This job meant the world to her.

"I don't expect you to be bosom buddies," Clyde said. "Getting along shouldn't be that difficult. If you didn't work so hard at disliking each other, you might discover you have several things in common."

"I doubt that." Frankly, Carrie couldn't see how it would be possible for them to agree about anything. She was twenty-seven, with limited radio experience. Finding another plum morning position, especially in the Kansas City metropolitan area, would be difficult. All right, it would be next to impossible.

"May I go now?" Carrie asked weakly. She stood, her shoulders slumped forward with the weight of her troubles.

"I've already spoken to Kyle," Clyde said as she moved toward the door.

"What did he say?"

Clyde rubbed his hand along the back of his neck. "His reaction was about the same as yours. He was shocked."

"I see."

"He wants to talk to you, OK?"

She blinked at him from the doorway. "What choice do I have?"

Clyde set his cigar in a crystal ashtray. "None. Really, it's a shame you can't get along," he muttered. "You're both hard-working, decent people."

Carrie hadn't gone more than ten feet down the long, narrow hallway that led to her tiny office when she came face to face with Kyle Harris. Neither spoke for several long moments.

Carrie tried to think of something witty, but her brain had deserted her. For someone known for her quick repartee, this was serious.

She looked up at Kyle, who towered a full eight inches above her, and tried to view him from a fresh perspective. His shoulders were broad and tapered down to lean hips and a flat stomach. From the office scuttlebutt she understood he kept trim with regular exercise. He often participated in ten-K fun runs, sometimes to benefit charity.

Carrie hated exercise. If ever she was tempted to join an aerobics class, she would lie down and take a nap until the notion passed.

Kyle's dark, intense eyes were studying her as thoroughly as she was him.

Someday Soon

Cain McClellan gets a thrill walking on the dangerous side of life. The bigger the risk, the greater the rush. Compared to the rush of taking on terrorists, love seems trivial . . . until he glimpses the delicate beauty of Linette Collins. Falling in love with Linette takes Cain by surprise, and before he knows it, he's utterly devoted to the angelic enchantress. But happily-ever-after doesn't come so easily for Linette. Already dealing with loss, she can't bear the thought of the danger Cain faces daily. Now Cain must choose: the danger he craves or the woman he loves?

CAIN NEEDED TO DO SOME CHRISTMAS SHOPping. That was why he'd come to Fisherman's Wharf. At least that was the excuse he'd used when he found himself wandering aimlessly along the waterfront.

The harder he worked to convince himself his being there had nothing to do with Linette Collins, the more obvious the truth became. He could have arranged for near anything he wanted over the Internet with little more than a credit card and a catalog number.

The only reason he was on the wharf was the ridiculous hope he'd catch a glimpse of Linette. Just one. Without her knowing. Why he found it so necessary to spy on her, he didn't know. Didn't want to know.

As it happened, he located her yarn shop tucked in a corner along Pier 39, the window display as charming and inviting as the woman herself. He stood outside several moments, his hands buried in his lambskin-lined jacket.

Uncomfortable emotions came at him like

poisoned darts, infecting him with all the might-have-beens in his life. He'd chosen this lifestyle, thrived on the challenge. No drug could produce the physical or emotional high of a successfully completed mission. No drug and no woman.

Then why was he standing in the cold like a lovelorn teenager, hoping for a glimpse of a widow he'd met briefly one night at a Christmas party? Clearly there were a few screws loose. The military had a word for this: battle fatigue. What he needed was a few uninterrupted days by himself to put his life back in the proper perspective.

Montana. Christmas was the perfect excuse to escape for a few days. It was long past time that he visited his ranch. He heard from the foreman he'd hired every now and again, but it had been well over a year since Cain had last visited the five-thousand-acre spread.

His strides filled with purpose, he walked along the pier until he saw a sign for World Wide Travel. After stepping inside the agency, he moved to the counter and waited his turn. A smartly dressed professional greeted him with a smile and arranged for his airline ticket to Helena, Montana. The only seats available were in first class, but Cain could well afford the extravagance. It was a small price to pay to escape San Francisco and the beautiful widow who'd captured his mind.

Experiencing a small sense of satisfaction, Cain tucked the airline ticket into the inside pocket of his jacket and continued on his way, moving down the waterfront and farther away from Linette. Farther away from temptation.

He was just beginning to think he had this minor curiosity licked when out of the blue, he saw her. For a moment it felt as if someone had inadvertently hit him against the back of the head. He went stock-still.

From the way her shoulders hunched forward he could see that she was tired. She stood in line at a fish and chips place, working to open the clasp of her shoulder bag. The wind whipped her hair about her face, and she lifted a finger to wrap a thick strand of dark hair around her ear.

The smart thing to do was to turn around, without delay, and walk away as fast as his feet would carry him. He'd gotten what he wanted. One last look at her, without her knowing. His curiosity should be satisfied.

Even as his mind formulated the thought, Cain knew just seeing Linette again wasn't nearly enough. He wanted to talk to her and get to know her. He wanted to sit down across a table from her and discover what it was about her that made a man who'd built his life around pride and discipline risk making a world-class fool of himself.

Sooner or Later

Rugged mercenary Shaun Murphy has everything he needs: the fortune, the attitude, and the evasive nature to stay just below the radar. So when Letty Madden, a Texas postmistress, tracks him down and begs him to help her find her twin brother, Murphy is less than enthused. Not needing monetary gain from this mission, he tries to scare Letty off by requesting a *different* kind of payment: one night in his bed. But it's going to take a lot more than that to repel this headstrong gal who's determined to find her brother, even if it means convincing this arrogant alpha male she'll go along with his plan. But neither one expected the sparks that would soon fly—and now getting out alive is the least of Murphy's worries.

I'M WILLING TO PAY YOU FOR YOUR SERVICES."

"Let me see if I understand you correctly," Murphy said, eyeing the prim and oh-so-proper postmistress who held his mail hostage. "You want *me* to accompany you to Zarcero?"

The woman was nuts, Murphy decided. There were no two ways about it. Letty Madden, postmistress of Boothill, Texas, was a prime candidate for the loony bin.

She looked up at him from behind her scarred oak desk in her private office, her brown eyes as dark as bittersweet chocolate. This female-in-distress performance might weaken another man's defenses, but not Murphy's. He had no intention of interrupting a well-deserved rest for some woman with an itch up her butt, seeking adventure.

His opinion of the opposite sex had never been high, and since his friends Cain and Mallory had both married, his attitude was even worse. It'd take more than the fluttering of this postmistress's eyelashes for him to traipse through some jungle on a wild-goose chase.

"You don't understand," she insisted.

Murphy understood all right; he just didn't happen to be interested in the job. Besides, the postmistress wouldn't earn enough money in two lifetimes to afford him or the services of Deliverance Company.

"It's my brother," she continued, and bit into her trembling lower lip.

A nice touch, Murphy mused skeptically, but it wouldn't change his mind.

"He's a missionary."

She actually managed to look as though she were on the verge of weeping. She was good, Murphy gave her that much. Sincerity all but oozed from her pores.

"Since the Zarceran government collapsed, no one in the State Department or CIA can tell me what's happened to him. The phone lines are down, and now the United States has severed diplomatic relations. The people in the State Department won't even talk to me anymore. But I refuse to forget my brother."

"I can't help you." He didn't mean to be rude, or heartless, but he simply wasn't interested.

He'd already told her as much three times, but she'd apparently opted not to believe him.

This was the first of several errors on her part. Murphy was a man who meant what he said. If her brother was stupid enough to plant himself in a country on the verge of political collapse, then he deserved what he got.

"Please," she added with a soft, breathless quality to her voice, "won't you reconsider?"

Murphy heaved an impatient sigh. The last thing he'd expected when he stopped off to retrieve his mail was to be cornered by one of Boothill's most virtuous citizens.

"You can help me," she insisted, her voice elevating with entreaty. "It's just that you won't. It isn't as if I'm asking you to do this out of the kindness of your heart!"

Good thing, because Murphy's nature didn't lean toward the charitable.

"I said I'd pay you, and I meant it. I realize a man of your expertise doesn't come cheap, and—"

"My expertise?" No one in Boothill knew what he did for a living, and that was the way he wanted it.

"You don't honestly think I don't know

what you are, do you?" Her chin came up a notch, as if he'd insulted her intelligence. "I'm not stupid, Mr. Murphy. There are certain matters one cannot help but notice when sorting the mail. You're a soldier of fortune."

She said the words as though they made her mouth dirty. No doubt this lily white sister of a missionary had never sunk to such despicable levels before now. Murphy, lowlife that he was, loved it. He certainly didn't expect a decent, God-fearing woman like Letty Madden would encourage business dealings with the likes of him.

"I'll pay you," she offered again. "Anything you ask."